PRINTHOUSE BOOKS PRESENTS

I0639249

Black Tie

One Heart, Three Lovers!
Drama, Fiction

Jara Everett

©2015, Jara Everett

Editor: Che' Y Middlebrooks

Publication date: 2-14-2015

PrintHouse Books, Atlanta, GA.

www.PrintHouseBooks.com

VIP INK Publishing Group, Incorporated

Cover art, designed by SK7

ISBN: 978-0-9861-340-0-5

Library of Congress Cataloging-in-Publication Data

Jara Everett

Black Tie: *One Heart, Three Lovers*/ Jara Everett

1. Drama 2. Thriller 3.Romance 4.Fiction
5. Jara Everett

Printed in the United States of America

A hot suspenseful romantic thriller about the life of Vivian Carter; a woman who loved her man more than anything in this world but that would all change when death comes knocking and separates their souls. Vivian develops a threatening disease and almost gives up hope, until she realizes she may have a second chance at life and this time Vivian was going to make it amazing. But could she love another as much as the man she so dearly cherished and lost.

I thank God, for my family, wisdom, strength, health and blessings he has graced me and my family with. To my husband and children I am blessed to be a part of your life. My dear cousin; Tillman Clayborne Stallion, R.I.P.

Table of Contents

CHAPTER 1

INDESCENT BEHAVIOR

My Story

IT was the middle of November. On a cold, rainy night in Chicago. I had 4 shots of Tequila and I was dying to get to my man's condo to see why he was ignoring my calls. Of course during the holiday season, traffic in the downtown area is crowded because every mother, grandmother and child are out doing last minute shopping which make people like myself very impatient. My goodness, I was dying of anxiousness to get to where I was going and the taxi driver didn't speak a lick of English. Why do they have people working in this country when they don't speak English?

I was so out of luck trying to ask the taxi driver why traffic was being held up. So I rolled the window down and ask a big husky guy driving a big eighteen wheeler if he could hear anything on his radio about what was holding up traffic.

When he said it was an accident a mile up, I knew then I had to foot it to my man's place. All I know is that I'm crazy about this dude and nothing else matter at this point. The only thing that matters to me is getting over to his place to find out why he's been ignoring my calls for the past few hours.

Hearing road raged drivers blow their car horns didn't make the situation any better. What the hell are they blowing for? Traffic can't move because the police think they own the world and has blocked the traffic.

Finally, I asked the driver to let me out of his car and to give me my total. He started saying something in his Arabic language like I was supposed to know what he was saying. His meter on the dash read sixty dollars. That's half of my insurance payment hell; I should've driven my own damn car or even caught the train.

But I was looking to cute to be on anybody's train. I felt and looked like a queen that night.

After I reached in my purse and gave the Arabic taxi driver my sixty dollars, he said something else to me. Then he waved the money as if he was complaining. After a few seconds, I realized he was complaining because I didn't tip him. A tip for what...I had already paid sixty dollars and I had to walk the rest of the way to my man's place. So I told him I will give him a tip alright. My tip to you is, learn how to speak English. I don't believe in tipping no one because to me, it's like giving away free money. If you're working a job that pays less because the boss want people to tip you then you shouldn't be working that particular job. That's how I see it.

One day I had a waiter quit on the spot because I would eat at this particular restaurant three days a week and those days happen to fall on his work days. The poor guy refuse to serve me and the boss told him he had to serve me or leave. So he left and said he quit because he served me well each time and I would never leave a tip for him. So with that being said, if I don't tip someone who has fed me, I for certain won't tip a taxi driver. Anyways, when I closed the taxi door the driver was still saying something to me with a roar in his voice and waving his hands. I did tell him to enjoy the rest of his day. The taxi driver might not know how to speak English but he, manage to use the "F" word and gave me, the middle finger. That word never bothered me.

What did bother me was as soon as I paid the taxi driver the traffic started moving ahead. Had I been more patient and waited a little longer, I would have been in that taxi and wouldn't have to worry about walking five blocks in five inch heels. Then the crazy thought of my man having another woman in his place gave me the energy to walk like a crazy woman in my sexy heels.

After I had walked the first block I looked around to see if another taxi was coming. I had no luck at all with catching another taxi. Then, by the time I had walked the second block, you best to believe them toes of mine had started to ache. Not only was my toes aching, the rain had started to drizzle even more. My poor feet sure had a challenge. They ached so bad, I walked passed people with a big old smile on my face to keep from crying and showing how much pain I was in. The smile on my face never dropped. It stayed the same. So people thought I was being friendly and smiling at them as we passed each other.

By the end of the forth block I looked at my man's building and stood there for a second. My feet were on fire. I took the shoes off and walked bare all the way to his door step and believe me, it felt as if I was soaking in a hot bath it felt so good to kick those heels off. The bad part about that was, I had to put the shoes back on in order to be cute again. The bottom of my feet, were gritty and dirty. I brushed my feet off and put my shoes on as if it was nothing. Look at the extent a woman would go through when she loves her man and I loved my man.

Inside my man's condo

I thought about him not answering my call again and it helped ease the pain. When I got inside of the lobby area my heart started beating faster which I thought, gave me even more energy.

I had made it to the lobby but I was thinking how in the hell am I going to get up to my man's floor without an elevator key to operate the elevator. Then a little elderly lady came in and used her key for the elevator. The elderly woman got off a floor before I was to get off on. When the elevator approached my man's floor, I quietly got off and walked up to his door. I used my cell phone to call my man once more to see if he would answer and again my man didn't answer his phone. I got desperate, and all I could think about was suppose he wouldn't open the door for me. Well, I'm from the hood, a smart woman I am. I know how to make ways and get through. So I did what I knew how and that was, pick his lock with my credit card. His lock was easy to pick because the dead bolt wasn't locked. If my man Tie had locked the dead bolt I might have been in trouble. So I open the door slightly and brushed my way in. I heard soft music playing. Talking about a heartbeat, heck, I had to remember how to breathe because now I'm convinced man is with another woman now. Soft music playing and he wasn't picking up his cell phone. I said forget about tip toeing. I went straight into his bedroom and bust through his door. There my man was sitting in the chair next to his bed and all he did was smile at me. I couldn't smile back, I wanted to know what was his problem ignoring my calls. My man was sure calm about the whole thing. He got up from the chair and said *"baby, I just wanted to see just how much I mean to you."* A part of me was still unsure and unclear about what he was saying because all I was thinking was, a woman could have just left and he was trying to play it off. He wanted to know how I got in and I told him I was taught well how to get into any place when I wanted in. He laughed at me and said; *"that's my girl, I knew all along you could handle yourself"*. It wasn't that easy for me to buy what my man was selling me, so I ask him to tell me why he didn't answer my calls and give it to me straight. My man was too busy trying to pull me close to him to kiss me. He grabbed me by the hands and took me to his balcony where there was a table filled with red roses, a bottle of imported red wine, to go along with the steak dinner hidden under the tray. I wanted to think all of the romance he had going on was for me but it was hard to believe. I mean, how he even knew I was coming over like a crazy person and I didn't have much time to wonder about it. Before you knew it, my man had pulled the chair out from the table and I sat down like a little helpless person. Boy, I felt gullible.

My man sat across from me, pulled his napkin out then placed it on his lap. Even looking at me with his sexy eyes turned me on.

I noticed a Neiman Marcus shopping bag next to my legs. Before he told me to look inside of the bag I was already two steps ahead of him, looking inside of the bag anyway. Its' for you he said. Still, he had me wondering why he couldn't just call me up and ask me over for a sexy dinner on the balcony.   For sure I was in doubt. What helped me feel better was when I opened the card I got from the bag and my name was labeled on it with such a sweet message. I felt real little. One thing for sure if he didn't know I was crazy over him before, I had no doubt that he was convinced now.

Remembering how extra my man would be at times and I mean, an over achiever in everything he sat out to do, I just went with the flow from that point on.

Inside of the bag was a beautiful dress. Now I had been in my man's life and for him to tell me that he would die over me and that was his love level for me, why wasn't I picking up a ring to go on my finger to go along with that crazy, romantic, weird dinner? What did a girl have to do to get her man to know that? Show me more is what I was really feeling.   Then, just when I was heading to the degree of conversation, he politely asked me to silence myself and to allow him.   Allow you what, more time to ask me to marry you. Hell, it had been five years already.

My energy level was getting impatient again so before things went left field my man grabbed my hands from across the table. I was about to say something to him about it but he interrupted my thoughts and reached across the table to grab my hands. Then he asked me to close my eyes so I did. He leaned over and kissed me. As soon as his tongue touched mine is when I felt the ring. My antennas raised and my estate was much higher. That's all I wanted from my man. I had five years, one month, six days, three hours and thirty-two minutes with my man's life. You damn right I was happy. What woman wouldn't be happy to marry a man that she has invested use of her body, mind, soul and eighty five percent of her time in. He asked me if I liked the ring. Honey, liked was an understatement. I could have swung from chandeliers that night. I loved it! I loved it more after he asked me to marry him. Before he could get the words out fast enough I said I do. The hell with finishing the sentence at that moment I helped him out where he didn't have to burn any more calories by finishing the word off with marry me because I stopped him at "will you" and said, hell yeah!

Waking up at the hospital

I was awake by the sound of the nurse and the doctor's voice. Although I was dreaming, it was one of those reminiscing moments I had. All I wanted to do was to fall back into that moment of me reminiscing that night on the balcony. But my mind wouldn't let me rest there again in that happy moment.

It took me a minute to realize where I was until I laid eyes on my man lifeless body on that hospital bed with all type of tubes in him. It a terrible thing to watch someone you love to rely on a life support machine because all you do is think about nature against science.

I saw the doctor taking his blood pressure and doing movement with his legs. I tried to listen to hear something different. Hopefully, good news. But there was no change in my man condition. Then after the nurse took my man vitals signs she left out with the doctor still talking softly between the two of them, I had all ears open to something positive with my man. When the nurse and my man doctor left, I got up and went over to his bedside. Trying to be strong for my man, I would crack a smile but deep inside I was in much pain. I have heard that a comatose patient could hear when a person speaks to them.

So I told my man how much I loved him. Every word that came from my mouth was good things. I even apologized for all of the negative energy I brought into our life.

As I was having my moment alone with my man, it wasn't long before I heard his loud mouth parents voice from the hallway. Like always, his mother was cursing his father. Some things never changes. I have never known anyone who's been married for over thirty years and they still have to clown. With his parents, if his dad says yes, his mother says no. When his mother says yes, his dad says no. Joanne and Frank could never agree on anything. I wonder if they could agree on sex. Like if Joanne would say, honey let me ride the surfboard would Frank say yes, or would he say no, let me hit it doggie style and then they debate for fifteen minutes on which position to have sex. That is how extreme those two were. Either they truly loved each other or they were nuttier than me. I guess everybody have to live their life the way they see fit.

I know I'm missing a few screws but I'm still a clever woman. Smart enough to know to prepare myself for when those two came inside the ICU room. Like always, I didn't have time for their nonsense but as the old saying goes…respect the elderly. Although, my man parents didn't know what respect meant. But all of that went out of the window when I saw my man poor mother grief over her son. Sitting there watching her as she wept over my man made me wonder just how much would a mother love her kid. I guess I would have to have a kid in order to find out. My mother left when I was a kid and still to this day, I wouldn't know what she looks like if she walked passed me.

Now Frank on the other hand was a character. A true meaning of the word, "hillbilly" who didn't care about what anybody thought of him. He also did whatever Frank wanted to do whether it was appropriate or in appropriate. He proved it to when he pulled out a can of beer from his shirt pocket while sitting in the chair next inside of the hospital next to my man bed. Not one bit was I surprised. Nothing, those country hillbillies did surprise me.

Even though Joanne was a hillbilly, she had standards…somewhat, because the next thing I heard was Joanne saying: " You're doing it anyway huh Frank?" She was a bit upset with Frank drinking beer in the hospital where their son was laying to rest.

Frank never liked Joanne to call him out with his habit so he retaliated by telling Joanne that he doesn't get on her when she goes to the gambling casino and spends up half of his money.

Now, they were doing all of this badgering with each other and neither of them had acknowledged that me being in the room. I think I even said hello at one point but they were so busy back and forth at each other throat that no one heard me.

Me knowing how my man parents were, I had learned to stay out of any encounter with those two because the moment you say something you might become a target and Frank wasn't hearing nothing Joanne was saying.

He waved his hand at her and told her to pay attention to their son and not him so much. Then he began sucking the foam from the top of the beer can. Joanne got so mad she started swearing at him. Calling Frank an alcoholic with sperm and got her pregnant. She even moaned about how she had the opportunity to be a model or to marry President Obama but instead she ended up with a long tall skinny waste man.

You would think that those types of words would tear any man down but not Frank. He was so used to the Joanne's verbally abusing him that it was normal. He even told Joanne that he needed that from her because since she don't give him sex anymore it makes him jerk off whenever he think about the mean words that comes from her mouth.

Joanne got stirred up more and the next thing I heard from Frank was, "all hell woman, you moan about anything". Frank shouted at Joanne to say that he might be a drunk but he was the breadwinner and took care of her very well for years. Then he called her lazy and they were going on and on. I definitely played my role by staying the hell out of it.

After a minute they calm down and Joanne rubbed my man face with a towel and told him to rest on, calling my man her baby. What she say that for…Frank never liked for Joanne to refer to their son as "baby" because it stirs Frank up for a different argument. Not because Frank starts the argument, it's because Joanne doesn't like for no one to tell her that her son isn't her baby. So there they were again, back at each other throat. WTF is all I was thinking. Give up already one of you. It was hard to sit there and listen to them go back and forth about not to call my man a baby, or Joanne telling Frank how he wasn't home much because he was too busy with his mistresses.

Now the mistress's part caught my attention because I didn't know that daddy Frank got down like that. He blamed Joanne for have allusions of him having mistresses because sometimes worked seventy hours a week. After a few minutes the nurse had no choice but to come in the hospital room to mainly shut those two up. Little did the nurse know, she saved me also from all of that negative energy? I tell ya, folks with negative energy can sure drain the hell out of ya. Even the nurse was drained because she had to come in and police those two, asking them to calm their voices or they would have to leave.

I was thinking to myself…don't the nurse sees Frank with a can of beer. Well, if she hadn't

Frank brought the fact of him drinking a beer to her attention by asking her when was their son going to get those tubes removed from him.

The nurse was in shock to see such nerve of a person to drink beer in a hospital and especially in the ICU. But she quickly solved that issue by telling Frank that the hospital has a rule of no alcohol allowed. Frank said, "my bad sugar" and told her he would pour the liquor out. Frank didn't have to pour it out because the nurse took the can away from him and took the other can from table. She told Frank that if he would pull another stunt like that that she would personally see to it that he won't have the privilege to step foot in the ICU again.

Frank apologized and Joanne told Frank that he should be sorry". Although their voices were a lot lower, I tuned them out and started reminiscing about time when first met my man at his office.

CHAPTER 2

THE OFFICE PLACE

Reminiscing the office place

I was hired as an administrative assistant at a Top Ten Advertising Agency in Chicago, Illinois. It was there, I saw my man for the first time. He had a lot of charm. But before I met my man that day at the office, I was taken on a tour by the office manager Greg.

I could tell that Greg was a little fruity from the moment he opened his mouth. Didn't bother me at all. I get along with gays just fine. I prefer a gay man as my acquaintance over a trifling woman. Greg walked me around the office introducing me to employees and giving me heads up on who's who.

Boy I tell ya, there were some good looking men working at that company. Some of them were looking so fresh it was hard to concentrate on anything else.   Where ever I would turn to, there was a good looking man around. Well dressed, groomed like they just stepped out of a G-Q Magazine. I said the hell with look like Suzie from nowhere... I have to step my game up a notch.   Even the receptionist was on point. She didn't have the looks of a beauty queen but she dressed like she had Oprah's money.

I just adored Greg.   He was so good at introduction. I felt like I was entertained by watching him perform as he introduced me to other employees because he was so dramatic with the way conducted his introductions.   It was a little bitchy at times but he kept my interest when he started to tell me everybody's business in the company.   I had learned that Sylvia, the receptionist was demoted to answering phones because she had supposedly screwed around with the VP of Sales name Charles Rosserio. Charles wife family was a big client of the agency and we know how the rest goes with that type of story.

Greg said that it wasn't fair, but who can prove that was the real reason because the sales department she worked under used lack of duty fulfillment for a reason to demote her. I didn't even know her but I felt bad for her because Greg said that Sylvia had to support five kids and they all have different fathers and the last baby daddy was locked up in prison for arm robbery. Greg didn't give me a chance to feel bad for long for her because he said she had a real stank attitude some days. Well, so do I. I just knew how to not show mine most of the time. I said, a glass of wine a day, takes the madness away. Greg gave me twirl and said hello with a crisp finger snap.

Then he went on and introduced me to Pat Irving. Pat was just hanging up from a phone call when we brushed passed her office. But she was more than delighted to welcome me into the company. Pat was beautiful. She was a stunning red hair woman with beautiful green eyes and tall like model. Pat said that I would enjoy working with her team because she wasn't lazy like some of the other VP's who wants their assistant to do all of their work for them. She did inform me that she wasn't to good at booking her own travel and especially, international travels because the airlines would always give her a reservation agent who barely speaks English and its hard for her to understand their accent. I assured her she would have no worry at all and that I could handle all of the travel she need. I could tell she was relieved to know that I was always willing to try.

When we left her presence Greg gave me a funny look and I asked him why. He said, *"trust me you don't want to know because I could go on and on about everybody up in here and every thing that I tell you miss thang, you can for sure take it to the bank."*

Well, I knew then that I would enjoy working at the agency because Greg would keep me up on folks business and that would make the time go by faster for me to work. Out of a good hour, I had learned of half of the company's employees business. I knew that Greg couldn't keep a secret if you paid him to.

He said as beautiful as Pat Irving is, she likes more honeys than bees can produce. I asked him how did he know so much of people business. He told me to stick around long enough. I will know everybody's business to and they will know mine.

A few offices down, we stepped into my man office. I could smell the cologne from the doorway. The rasp in his voice also caught my attention. My man didn't hear us come in his office because he was on the phone with his back turned toward us. That was fine by me. There, I had the chance to check my man out from head to toe without him knowing I was checking him out. I know what I like when I see it and I was highly interested.

After my man hung up the phone, he turned around with a bright confident smile. Then Greg introduced me to him as his New Administrative Assistant. He was pleased to meet me and I was even more pleased to meet him.

Although I had never worked at an advertising agency before, I felt that I could jump right in as if I had worked for an advertising agency for years. A least that what I told my man. It didn't matter to him. All that mattered was for me being a fast learner and a multitasker.

My man smiled and welcomed me to the company. He was happy to have an assistant but he said that he hated the fact of sharing his assistant with three other VP's in the company because he has to present a lot of Presentations. With that charm and that smile, my man for sure didn't have to worry.

I could have talked him for an hour but I had other two more VP's to meet.

Since Greg was the man who knew everybody's life story I had to ask him my man story. But Greg didn't have a story on my man. He thought my man life was too boring and my man possessed such a by the rules and regulations attitude. If you wasn't about drama Greg wasn't interested. And my man being seen with his momma only, out of the seven years he had been with that Agency, wasn't enough to keep Greg's interest in wanting to know about his life.

Well, I was soon to solve that no interest Greg spoke about pertaining to my man. My mind was set on getting my man and turning him from a no interest at all into a Celebrity Status type interest. You better believe I took the first shuttle into space!

Meanwhile, Greg and I walked and talked. While meeting others at the company, I thought about ways I could get my man to notice me. I was thinking to do something like wear an almost borderline skirt with no panties underneath. Drop a pen on the floor and then bend over to pick it up. Or, I could just walk pass his office fifty times in one day. Even I had to scratch my own head to think of that one. I could be viewed as a psycho to walk pass his office fifty times in one day and that would turn my chances off for sure. However; I knew I had it in me to pull him.

Any thought was a good thought as far as I was concerned. But the best thing was knowing I had to go into his office and pick up his scribbles and turn it into a presentation.

I could tell that Greg knew what I was up to. Well I am far away from being anybody's fool. Although my man didn't have a woman at that time, I knew that I would have to take a number and probably steal my way to the front of the line to get in. Besides, I had a better chance anyway. I was fresh filet minion fresh off the grill and those other women on the job were pan, refried rib eyes.

I always had a way of getting what it was I wanted. If I wanted it, I would waste no time on getting it. Growing up in the hoot taught me that if you snooze you lose. That's not always the case but when it comes to competition I raised the bar.

When I told Greg my thoughts and how I would get my man, he said not to hold my breathe because a few of the other women have said the same thing and he had to help them pick their bottom jaw up from the floor.

He didn't have to worry about picking my bottom jaw up because it welded together well.

After Greg saw that fire coming from inside of me, he and I became real good friends from that moment on. We got along just fine.

Later on that afternoon, my man walked out of his office. With him was a male co worker. In passing, He walked near me and I looked at him in his eyes as if I was in a daze. His coworker was checking me out but I hardly noticed his coworker my eyes were solely on my man.

Back in my man room at the hospital

I haven't reminisced that moment of me and my man life for a while. I was quite enjoying being back in that moment. That is until I felt Greg aggressively shaking me to wake up from my sleep.

I had to let him know that he woke me up at the wrong time. I was just reliving me and my man moment of when we met.

Greg seemed to be a little concerned about me because it took a minute for me to realize I was still sitting by my man bedside. By the time Greg had made it to the hospital, I was looking tired and feeling a little fatigue even though I told him that I was feeling okay.

I was probably looking tired to because the past few days I had been sleeping in the chair next to my man bedside waiting on him to wake up.

Greg sat some beautiful roses on the table. Its was touching to see him caring about my man so much and me. We had gotten so close in the short length of time I had worked at the Advertising Agency.

Greg looked really happy. He wanted to bring some life into the room. So he opened the curtains. Then he said to me, *"Honey, if you need your man to wake up you need some life up in here, sunlight brings energy. You got this man up in here in this dark dingy room."*

Then he walked out of the room to grab some scissors. When he came back in the room he started cutting the stem from the flowers. He asked me how many days have I been there. I told him it's been two day.

For me, it didn't matter if I had been there all week. As long as the hospital had a place for me to wash my tale, I was good.

At that time, Greg had become a dear friend of mine and I knew that Greg wanted my man to escape that COMA just as much I wanted him to escape it.

Greg convinced me to leave the hospital and go out with him for lunch and that wasn't a bad idea. We left the hospital to have a sit down at lunch and to do some girl talk.

I wanted my man Tie to wake up but I couldn't help but to think about what it would do to me if my man would wake up and I'm not there by his side.

But trying to judge when my man would wake up would be a long shot for me. So, I decided it wasn't a bad idea to go to lunch with Greg since he did come so far to see my man and to check up on me.

Having a lunch with a good friend.

Greg and I stopped over at Nordstrom to have lunch there. It was one of our favorite spots to grab a good quick lunch. Greg was so funny because whenever we would go out to eat he would order two meals just so he could have a variety of food to eat. I used to hate it when he would order his food because he would put so much drama in expressing how he wanted his meal prepared. I would warn him not to piss the server off. It was bad enough that I never would tip them.

Greg wanted to order a bottle of sweet wine. Not knowing which wine on the list to order, he told the waitress to choose and make sure that the wine was as sweet as the guy who was sitting across the table on the opposite side of where he and I was sitting.

Then he waved at the guy. I just looked to the ceiling for a second. Greg wanted me to join in the alluring moment but I wasn't in the mood to stand for his gay adventures and I had to tell him.

I had a sudden fever or down moment. Watching people there at the restaurant as a couple made me feel sad. All I was thinking about was how my man and I were out eating just before he fell ill.

After a few words later came the cry like a river tears flowing down my face. Good I didn't have my face beat that day otherwise that would have been a scary sight to have black eye liner mixed in with concealer running down the side of my face. I was way too cute to look like scary Mary.

All I know is, I needed my man. He was the other half of my brain. I asked Greg, have you ever loved anybody so much that your chest hurt when you can't be with them?

Greg never gave me a straight answer but he did say that I seemed different.

That's because I loved my man and I wanted nothing else more. He suggested to take me home or to be around family during that time of triumph. He also thought it was not normal to be inside of that hospital room for almost three days and not go home or even get fresh air.

Then he went on to tell me about his cousin who went crazy because she worried her self to death when her husband died.

Well, I might have been down at that moment. But I wasn't to down to know that my man was alive. So that was no comparison.

Although Greg wasn't saying everything right, I could tell that he felt my cry.

Moments after, the waitress came back to the table to serve us the bottle of wine. . The wine was tasteful. It made me think about when my man and I would go out to dinner together and enjoy a good wine.

Then I started to reminisce the time when we out of town together on a business trip attending a charity event.

Reminiscing, Charity Event with my man

Back then, I was still working as the assistant to my man. The company's clients were big donors or that particular charity event. The event was in honor of Breast Cancer Awareness.

A couple by the name of Deborah and Mark Valentino were big donors and they were the President of this particular Charity. They were also clients of the Agency.

That night I was on my third glass of wine. I was sitting next to the two most important people at the Charity Event. Mark and Deborah Valentino and while Mark was a happy go lucky man Deborah on the other hand enjoyed running her mouth about a bunch of nothing.

My man sat next to Mark and I sat next to Deborah who talked my ears off. Boy was I glad to drink some wine that night. One reason was because of the attraction I had for my man and we still worked tighter. The second reason was that I was hard to fight my feelings I had for him that night. I did not want it to be so obvious.

A least I knew how to control myself whenever I would drink. Deborah on the other hand did not. Her liquor intake was showing slowly through her speech and her actions. When you can't hear your own voice talking and everyone else could hear you just fine, that 's when you should call it quits.

Meanwhile, the host of the evening was speaking about the seriousness of Breast Cancer and how early diagnosis could help save millions.

Deborah had been a breast cancer survivor and she was living proof of catching the cancer early enough where treatment helped her to survive and beat the cancer. Being that early detection helped save her life, Deborah stays true to getting her annual screening.

Didn't mind her talking my ears off about beating the Breast Cancer for eight years. That was something worth listening to. She also mentioned how beating breast cancer brought her closer to God.

I don't judge no one but however and whatever brings you closer to the Lord is a step in a good direction for me.

She didn't just stop there with being thankful. She also praised her husband Mark on being the best husband in the World. To me, every woman has the best man in the world. If you don't think it, who else will?

She said that Mark was by her side every day and he made sure she had no situations around her where it would cause her stress.

Deborah looked at me and said, you know young lady, sex have been better than ever between Mark and me.

I damn near spilled my wine. It caught the attention of my man ear and Mark ears.

Deborah said that as if it was a normal casual conversation. My first time meeting that lady and here she is discussing her sex life about her husband. She really blew me away when she said that old Mark had an Anaconda.

Deborah was delighted to tell me that Mark being in his sixty's was a walking proof that just because your bones may lose it density and you will lose some muscles mass in certain areas, it doesn't necessarily mean that a man would lose muscle mass in his Anaconda.

Then she went on to say, out of twenty-five blessed years, she and her husband screw like young people. She leaned over closer to me, whispered in my ear and said, and he doesn't need to take Viagra to keep it going.

We were supposed to be at the charity event to represent our company which the agency were also donors, not be there to listen to two highly respected wealthy donors talk about their sex

like as life. I was being used as a sex therapist.
Mark and my man carried on conversing with
one another.   Moments later the host had
ended her speech and we all clapped. I didn't
get a chance to hear much of what the host was
speaking about because Deborah Valentino
had my attention pretty much the whole damn
time. I don't know what in the hell made her
think that I wanted to hear about her sex life
with a man damn near seventy years old.

I was still trying to get the man in front on
me…my man with his sexy tale.

I knew that Mark Valentino was used to his
foul mouth wife talking to anybody about sex
because he graced her behavior as if it was
normal. I had to clear my throat after Mark
shouted, his wife was a Beast in the bedroom
and that she loves to nibble.

I guess I was must have been a little loud
clearing my throat because Mark asked me if I
was all right.

Well, if he had stopped talking about sex maybe I would have been all right. Since he joined in with his wife in the sex talk, it made me a little moist between the legs only for my man, which I had eyes on since I'd been there that night. Mark acted as if it was a normal conversation for them to talk about sex so openly. I had to clear my throat because all this sex talk made me wonder about my man even more.

All I was thinking was, those two were made for each other. Mark took over from Deborah and said that big harry forest on her was still just as tight as the day he first entered in her.

My man and I looked at each other. He smiled at me and I smiled back. He wasn't interested in that nonsense sex talk from his client either. But you have to allow a fool with money the space to make a jackass out of his self. Usually when jackass like think they have more money than God you can't tell them nothing.

Mark noticed how my man and I looked at each other. He stopped talking about Deborah and asked my man to tell him about our sex life.

I laughed out loud, more   and strong years of marriage. Then Mark asked my man Tie what about his sex life with me.

I laughed out loud. Tie told Mark that we were just coworkers and I was his assistant and VP's of marketing assistant.

Mark wasn't buying us being just coworker only. He actually had a hard time believing my man wasn't tapping my behind while the doors were closed. He though it was great because he and Deborah met when she was his assistant.

Deborah cosigned with him. She told us to stop fooling ourselves because she could see the lust in our eyes. Even I cosigned that one because I know I was lusting for my man for a while now. You never had to tell a woman like me that life was to short not to do whatever I wanted to do. I had already had my mind made up that I was having my man that night.

My plan was to get my man all up inside of me.

I took another sip of that wine and place it down softly, gave my man that I want you look and it was time to unleash the dragon. That dragon was me huh. Tie knew exactly what time it was because his eye stayed on me. Even when he tried to convinced Deborah again that he and I were just coworkers.

Deborah didn't buy that sale. She said huh, that what your mouth say. Mark got her up from the table to dance leaving my man and I at the table with just the two of us.

I excused myself from the table. I gave my man a full view. He need to see me in my beautiful dress again and I had his whole attention as I walked away from that table. That night I was scoring high points.

The music was beautiful. It was one of Beethoven 's classics playing. I love the sound of classical while attending an evening of black tie events.

When I got to the women rest room, I powdered my face and looked at myself real good in the mirror. I was amazed with how beautiful I looked that night. How could a foster child hood girl pull a man like my Tie? When will the hood come out of me? Then I told myself to just be me and let the cards fall where they may. But no, I said to myself. I don't want to scare him off. I waited seven months already I could wait a little longer. But that other little voice overpowered my voice and gave me the level of confidence, I needed. That was to tell that man I wanted to be with him. Even, if it was one night only.

Insecurity sure will play on your mind at the wrong time. But I kicked insecurity to the curve that night. My man could swallow my salary if it was side by side with his but money ain't everything. Most men prefer to make more money anyways due to the fact that when a woman make more money than her man, usually she is harder to deal with. Most men like it easy with a woman. But that wasn't for me to worry about. My thing was patience and I had exercised enough of it. That was big for me to do.

As I walked back to the table, I saw my man standing up waiting for me. He asked me for a dance with him. Hel, I thought he would never ask.

So we danced and at first there was silence as we danced. My man asked me if I was enjoying the evening.

That was an understatement. I was elated.

Not knowing what he was thinking, I tilted my head to the side. He grabbed me by the chin and asked me if I was for sure, I was enjoying the evening. I said yes, I'm sure.

I asked my man if he was enjoying the evening. He said more than ever. He then went on to say he had waited for months to enjoy that night...with me.

I felt like I had just been shocked by a blast of energy. I actually felt my heart beat because he beat me to the punch. I said, come again?

Again, he said, I want to get out of here and be with the woman I am in love with.

The music stopped and there was complete silence. Before I got the word okay out he had kissed me on lip, soft and gentle.

I felt like a kid in a candy store. I felt so light on my feet. It felt like I weight about a hundred pounds. I didn't say look like it because I got to much booty for that. But that heavy weight of wanting to let my man know how I felt was over.

My man walked up to Mark and Deborah say their goodbyes and Deborah held her glass up to me and winked her eye.

Outside the even hall

The driver pulled up close that my man and I could get inside the car. All of heaven broke loose in the back seat.

At the hotel

The elevator couldn't close fast enough before we started kissing each other all over. I unzipped his pants, then pulled a condom out of my clutch and put it on him. He leaned me back on the elevator and raised my dress up. Then he lifted my leg and penetrated in side of me slowly. I wrapped my legs around him and I was lifted up higher.

As we approached the floor to get off, he put the elevator door to close the elevator to close the door.

I said, we should go inside the room. He said, right.

He zipped his pants and helped me fix my dress. He was still concern with how I was feeling. I told him I was just fine.

We didn't even have time to turn the light on in his hotel room before we were at it again. My man needed that comfort and it was destined for me to give it to him.

I took his black tie off and he picked me up with his strong arms and placed me on his bed. I wrapped his tie around my neck before we started kissing again.

All I had on was his black tie and he was completely nude. My man body was fit like he born from a fitness gym. I was so attracted to him that when he entered inside of me again I had to grab on tight to the sheets.

That time he had me bent over from the back. It felt so good I went from grabbing the sheets to biting the sheets just to keep my voice of pleasure from carrying into the next person room.

That moment was so good I didn't want it to end. While in the middle of our pleasurable moment, my man hit every spot that I didn't even know I had. We were both dripping in sweat and my hair was everywhere. We had an endearing moment of pure pleasure and before he made his final call, I showered him.

The next morning.

The next morning I woke up in my man arms. He held on to me tight so any movement I made he felt it. I realized I was still wearing his black necktie. He said that I wore his black necktie well.

My man felt it was important for me to know that I was special to him the first day that I stepped foot in his office. I had no idea he was keeping up with my world just as much as I was keeping up with his world.

I thought by his demeanor, my man had come from a family of wealth but shared with me how he had to work hard to get to the top level.

Its not about where you come from he said, its about where you're at now.

The next thing I felt was something shaking me hard.

Back at the restaurant inside Nordstrom

Then, I heard Greg's voice saying, *"child, do you know how many times I have heard this love story."*

Well, enough for feeling good for the moment. Greg blew my moment of reminiscing my love for my man.

Just because his chicken was seasoned right when the server brought his food to him didn't mean he had to blow my good moment. Then he had the nerves to say, blame it on the chef because he didn't use the proper season. I was like really, Greg.

The waitress brought the bill over to the table and Greg said he would pay for the lunch. He asked me to leave a tip and I had to remind him that I don't do tips.

Greg asked me, what he was going to do about me as if there was something wrong with me not tipping. I work all day, five days a week and no one tipped me. I feel that, folks with jobs where they are depending on tips should find another job.

Greg called me a mean girl. Call me what you want but I am who I am and I feel the way that I feel.

Greg thought my attitude had become a little feisty since my man had been ill. He was right. The only thing about it was, my attitude been feisty, I just tried not to show much of it unless it was necessary to show. I told him that we should get back to the hospital but he said he would catch me later.

CHAPTER 3

NOT ABOUT MEGAN

Back at the hospital

I left Nordstrom and walked back to the hospital. When I made it back to my man room my sister Angie and Megan was there in the room with him. It was nice to see my sisters showing support. They came to see how my man was doing and how I was holding up.

My younger sister Megan asked me if I wanted to go to lunch. I told her I had just eaten. My oldest sister asked me if I knew what was next with my man. What were the doctors saying? I told her the doctors said they were seeing if the medication would fight off the infection. His white blood cells weren't strong enough to heel himself.

They didn't want my Tie awake because it could risk his body being to stressed. My oldest sister prayed for my man. My younger sister never believed in prayer for someone to live. Megan believes that if God has a calling for you, its selfish for you to pray to keep him in the flesh.

So Megan told us that when we were done praying for my man to live when we don't know Gods plan for him to call her back in the room.

Angie said to overlook our little sister mouth. She's immature and her only concern is herself.

That little incident put me back into a memory of when the three of us was vacationing at Breckenridge Ski Resort before anyone knew my man was sick.

Although it was two years ago, it seemed like it was yesterday in those mountains. What a beautiful place we stayed at, Breckenridge Ski Resort. My first time ever visiting the resort. We all sat around drinking coffee and tea.

Although Breckenridge Ski Resort was beautiful, it was freezing cold.

I've always enjoyed inviting my sister Angie and Megan on trips with my man and I. Leave it up to those two; we wouldn't do anything because they rely on me to make all of the decisions on where to go.

Although Megan is a brat, she does bring excitement and drama. On the other hand, Angie is a little bit calm.

Miss Megan is about self only most of the time. But as longs as you know your family you can deal with them. The reason why I deal with Megan is the fact of her being my sister and I love her.

We were having quite an enjoyable evening. My brother-in-law Richard was a little annoyed because he wanted a beer and so did my man. The Weather was to bad and it was to late to order anything else. So the fellas had to drink what the ladies were drinking or stick to tea and coffee for the night. Regardless of how the others felt, my man and I were enjoying every moment we had with each other.

The whole time, my man couldn't keep his hands off of me. The touch of his hands felt good around my neck as he messaged it.

The eyes of the others were all over us. I was waiting for someone to say something. Angie being the funny one was the first one to open her mouth and call us out. I could tell by the look on her face she admired what my man was doing to me. Because she go on Richard about not giving her a neck message like my man was doing me. Richard said that he would romance his wife, rub her neck, her back and anything else she needed. All she had to do was day the word.

After Richard told Angie it was her world and he just wanted a piece of it, Angie buttered him up and gave him a kiss. Referring to Richard as her Sugar Plum Pumpkin.

 I never heard anyone use that term before.

Angie said that Richard loves showing out and didn't want anyone else to out beat him with romance.

Megan shouted out and said, Louis who was her fiancé at the time never even thought about giving her a rub, romance or nothing.

I was thinking, oh boy, here we go. I could tell by the tone of her voice that her glass of wine was working her brain.

Louis had to defend himself by saying he works all the time and he should be the one getting rubbed down because all Megan does is shop at expensive boutiques and run his credit accounts up. He also said she would never complain about that. Megan said, of course not because Louis knew she was a shopaholic before they got serious with each other and before he asked her to marry him.

Angie being likes to correct terms of speech with a person. So she says to Megan, "but you're not married yet honey. Get the ring first and then show him what you're really about".

"Ha" My man almost spilled his drink.

Richard didn't make it any better because he instigated the conversation. Trying to make it seem like that how we as women all operate. He thinks women have nothing else better to do with their men than to get men in a tight situation and then stick it to them.

Megan grabbed Louis by the Chen and not to worry about what was going on across form them because she knows they have a good thing.

I was thinking, yeah Megan, butter that man up because you know we will throw jumping cables on a man in a heartbeat.

Louis grinned like a big baby. Then Megan kissed Louis. Still buttering him up like she was buttering up a grandma homemade fluffy biscuit.

I couldn't hate on Megan though. We all have the tendency to butter our men up in the time of need. So I would have did what Megan had done...change the subject quick to get her man mind on something else.

Angie was no good for that one either. Making that man think that his woman weren't showing her true self. I kept watching Louis after all of that and he looked uncomfortable and stayed quiet the rest of the stay. So Kudos to my sister for making Angie talk about herself.

That night it felt like fireworks were going off. The conversations were starting to get real juicy

Started with Angie's great announcement about she and Richard were expecting a baby.

My eyes lit up. I was so excited to be an Ante soon. Each of us congratulated Richard and Angie on their pregnancy. Everyone accept Megan.

Again, Megan being a little brat brought tried to focus the attention back to herself.

I heard Megan say, better you than me. Ain't no little creatures coming from this body no time soon.

Then she asked Angie why would she want to get all fat and out of shape just to have a baby for a man who might not be there in the next few years.

I tried to stop her from running her mouth. Angie told me to let Megan have the floor. She wants her to feel like it's her show so she could make an ass out of herself.

Megan went on to say that she doesn't bite her tongue and that's what men do. Get the pretty women with nice bodies and bang them up with babies then don't want them when they bodies get all loose.

I asked Megan to just be happy for her sister and be happy that she will be an Ante.

Megan wasn't trying to hear nothing I was saying.

It was that night I learned that Megan was still upset with me for loving my man so much because she and I don't hang out nearly as much as we used to before I fell in love with my man.

Louis felt like he and Megan could spend more time since Angie was pregnant.

I thought it was great for Louis to feel that way. Megan didn't think so because she wouldn't stop running her mouth about it.

Suddenly she turned into a bull. Speaking to Louis in a very savvy way she says, *"why, so I could end up pregnant and pathetic looking like most pregnant women while they man is out screwing some jump off home wrecker with the perfect botched up body, not me Louis, no time soon so don't even think about it. We already had that discussion so if you think that's what we're going to do when we get married then we need to re think about this engagement shoot. I have already said, once were married, no babies for five years and we don't even have a date set for our marriage yet which buys me more time". That ain't cool.*

I though wow, how cold my sister is to her man at times. But he must like it to deal with her attitude.

Richard told her to calm down and his wife will be just as beautiful eight months pregnant and the way he feel about his wife, no ass can take that away from his family.

I know Richard loves his wife. If he would ever cheat on Angie, I would be totally shocked.

Megan still was turning her lip up like a kid. I don't know what became of her but she was a raging bull after that announcement.

Angie just sat there quietly with a little smile.

Now I understand why Angie used to say that some things are better left unsaid.

Megan was quick to talk again. Mainly trying to correct Richard and convince Angie that

Richard only talked about not leaving her and not that he won't cheat on her.

I held my head down because there was no giving up for miss know it all Megan

Richard said, *"Hey, that goes for cheating and everything else. I've been in this family for six years...I would think I deserve better respect from you Megan. I love your sister. We don't need you to worry about us over here. You worry about why you have had four unsuccessful engagements and are now on your fifth one over there. Sorry Louis."*

Richard kissed Angie and left the room.

Louis didn't blame Richard for reacting that way and responding to Megan. He actually agreed with Richard and decided that maybe He and Megan do need to re think some things. Louis had his last straw with Megan. He told her about her immaturity and rudeness and then let the room.

"Oh well, let the cards fall where they may." Is all that Megan had to say after Louis got up and left the room.

My man went to check up on Louis just to get pass this whole episode.

Megan was still talking and I told her to shut up. Angie told her she was way out of line and if she would ever disrespect her husband again in that manner that she would not be bothered with her at all.

Megan did apologize for her behavior. But it was a little late to be apologetic. I remembered one of our foster mothers would say to us to be careful on what you say and how you say it to people because words are something you can't take back and people will always remember words.

Next thing I heard was Megan crying on the couch like a ten year old. Angie rushed to her side to comfort her. I said to let her cry it out. She had too much to drink and didn't know how to control herself.

Although Megan felt sorry, there was nothing to excuse her for such a derogatory behavior.

Angie, like always stood by her side and comforted her. She knew I wasn't in it.

So that woke me up.

Back in hospital room

When I came back from dreaming of what happened previous in our life. Angie was still talking. Reminding me that Angie was our little sister and wanted me to remember that it has always been just the three of us. I understood all of that but I didn't mean I have to deal with Megan's attitude problem.

Angie reminded me that we have all problems and we all deal with it differently. I didn't challenge her with how she felt. That just wasn't the right time to deal with Megan's problems.

I said to Angie, I appreciate you coming to see my man, but please, understand that I am going through a lot of pain right now. For reasons you see and for reasons you don't have a clue of.

Angie isn't confrontational. When someone asks her to do something she just does. It.

Angie understood and said to call her if I needed anything.

I love both of my sisters dearly but I was too weak to deal with the drama.

When Angie left I went over to my man bedside and told him how much I miss him and how I couldn't wait until he came home.

Although I hated leaving, it was necessary for me to go home and take a good shower.

Then I thought I heard a moan from my man. Or I thought that maybe I was just hearing something because the room was silent with just the sound of the monitor.

Then suddenly the sound of the monitor started beeping faster. And I started to get worried. So I looked at the machine and it was beeping faster. His heart rate was to the roof.

The nurse and the doctor came inside the room. They asked me to step out of the room and they closed the door.

I peeked through the window and they got his heart rate back to normal.

Afterwards, the nurse came out and said that my man needed to rest and it would be a few hours before they would want him to have visitors.

The nurse tried to explain to me how sometimes a person in a coma could hear you but they can't move. I didn't need her to tell me something I kind of figured anyway.

I decided to take a break anyway and get back to me a little bit. The past two days I had let myself go. I was very tired. I slept sitting up in the chair for two day.

CHAPTER 4

AN UNCLEAN PAST

Needing a relief

I had finally gotten home. After two days, all I did was I was in need of a hot bath. I went straight to the bathroom to run me a tub bath.

I went to pull some underwear from the drawer and stated smelling my man t-shirts. Umm, his t-shirts had the smell of Kenneth Cole Cologne.

I stood in front of the mirror and took off my clothes.

I almost forgot the water was running in the tub. So I quickly went back into the bathroom to turn it off.

I turned off the cold valve but the hot valve wouldn't shut off. I had to use a lot of force to shut that hot valve off.

Still I couldn't get the hot valve to shut off. I used extra forced and finally the valve went off. In the process of shutting the valve off my earring fell in the tub.

I reached in the tub to get my earring and the water was to hot to keep my hand inside. Finally once the wave of the water settled in the tub I was able to get a clear view of my earring.

Although the water was steaming hot, I quickly put my hand in the hot tub of water again and grabbed my earring with the quickness.

That moment brought back memories of my man and I inside of the hot tub together.

Reminiscing the hot tub

My man was so romantic at times. That night was special because it was New Year's Eve. .

My man and I were both sitting in the hot tub when my earring fell out of my ear. Now supposedly, he was trying to feel for my earring under the water but somehow his hands kept going to my private area. He kept saying he felt my earring but each time it was goody goods.

I asked him to stop fooling around and to help me find my earring. He kept playing with me under the water and finally he got my earring for me out from underneath him.

I was sitting in front of him while he was caressing water with a sponge onto my top chest.

It was hard for me to believe that my man could be so loving and so real that he had been single all this time. He was truly my soul mate.

I asked him to tell me why he was single for so long. He said he didn't know. But if he had to guess, he was always shy and his social skills weren't that great on a personal level. Business level he rocked social skills.

Times have changed and things aren't like they used to be with a man a woman. Women are strong since the eighties. They come on to men faster than men have come on to them.

He didn't doubt how I felt about it. He just simply said that before me, no one caught his eye.

I was melting inside with love all over again. Even if he didn't mean what he was saying, it sure felt good. It felt so damn good to hear him say those words to me. I was falling deeper and deeper in love with my man.

I was glad that someone was stupid enough to let him go because everything that is good is in timing.

I just can't see why a woman would have cheated on a man like my man. He was super intelligent, smart, sex was all that and more, and he was what every woman needs from their man...a great financial provider.

But after he explained to me what he wanted in a woman and he found her in me. I had to tell him the whole truth about me. Well, I told him most of the truth about me.

But I let him finished first telling me more about his life. At that time, we had only been together for eight months. So I was still learning some things about my man.

At that time, my man told me the story of him being a policeman ten years before he and I had met. There was an incident one night that involved an armed robbery while he was on duty.

He and his partner took the call and it turned out to be a shootout that turned ugly. His partner, who was also his best friend, was shot and killed and he ended up shooting and killing the suspect in line of duty.

Although he ended up leaving the force, he still suffers some night and re lived the incident in his sleep at times.

He said that in his last relationship. His ex would use that against him and call him weak because he would wake her up in the middle of the night and needed to talk to her. She said that a real man would be strong, deal with it and go on. She said she was sick of hearing about my problems and that I should never have become a cop if I couldn't handle it.

He said that not only did she verbally abuse him at times, she was cheating with one of the other officers on the force and he happened to be her partner.

I guess some people are never happy with what they have until its gone because after he left her, she tried everything to get his heart back but it was too late. My man said that he didn't want to feel the constant heart break. He also said that women don't realize that men cry in the dark to.

So to get his sanity back Tie said that he took a long break to find himself in life and then years later is when I came along. That's when he felt good to love a woman again.

Although Tie said that he talked it out with a therapist, the hunting of the homicide never stopped hunting him until the first night I stayed with him at the hotel. That's when he knew I was right him.

I assured Tie that if he would ever awake from a bad a dream. I would hold him until he's ready for me to let him go.

His head leaned on my head and he kissed my forehead.

I told my man that my past wasn't pretty at all and one day I would share that with him.

My man didn't care about my past. He only wanted me to assure him that I was all his.

I assured him that I was all his, but that wasn't the whole truth. I couldn't tell him the whole truth about me after I had already won his heart of trust. I knew that I had to get my mess straighten fast because it was only a matter of time before the truth comes to hunt you.

Just as the truth hunted my man in his dreams, the truth was near to hunt me in the light.

My situation was a lot deeper. It wasn't taking someone's life but sad to say. I was still very well married, legally.

None of that oh we're married spiritually. No, I was married by the legal law govern under the United States of America.

I had only mentioned to him in the past about my ex man going away to prison. But I left that part out about my marriage to him.

I guess I tried to live a life in a big lie. Married and didn't want to deal with it.

My man asked me good, had I buried that past relationship, and I said yes. In my mind, I had buried my past relationship but legal documents said that he wasn't the past at all.

I was property of another man. That was truly not good. I couldn't blame anybody but myself. No matter what, I did not stand to lose my man.

No man has ever made me feel as good as my man made me feel.

I never told my man much about my ex man but I did tell him that I grew up in a foster care in the hood. That's was pretty much of all that he knew about me. He would always say that when I was ready to talk he would be willing to listen.

Well, I had come a long way from being involved in gangs and dating gangsters and drug dealers.

I figured, If I could get to my ex man and get him to sign divorce papers this process could be smooth sailing and my man would never have to know that I was never one hundred percent true with him.

On second thoughts, I could just convince my brother-in-law to sign my ex name on the divorce papers. But he was the type of Jamaican you didn't want to lie on. That was one of the prices I had to pay for dating a gangster.

A little time late I felt a little guilty but I knew I couldn't show my guilt. He had learned me enough to know when something was wrong with me. My man paid close attention to my every move.

So I had to pretend normal as I stood in the mirror and dried my body off. What did I see in me...a deceitful person trapped in a lie? I was honest with myself.

Right in the middle of me drying myself off, my man came up from behind and asked me to turn around.

He then put a necklace around my neck and said "Happy New Year's baby and happy one year anniversary to us as a couple". The necklace must have cost a fortune. I wasted no time in getting dressed so we could enjoy the night and bring in the New Years together.

Then suddenly, I was awakened from reminiscing by the sound of the doorbell.

Celebrating New Years Eve night

The doorbell rung and instantly I stopped day dreaming about me and my man tub bath together.   It was strange because when I went to open the door. No one was there.

The doorbell rang again. I went to answer the door and it was my girlfriend Lori. She had come to get me out of the house for New Years.

The first thing she said was she was worried about me because she hadn't heard from me since my man was in the hospital.

One reason I didn't answer calls or return phone call was simply the fact that I wasn't in the mood to talk.

Lori was my true friend and I knew I should have kept her in the loop with how I was feeling.   I barely would answer my sister's phone calls.

If you never loved anyone the way I loved my man, you would never have known what I must have going through.

I know I'm selfish at times especially when I don't tip servers but I do love my friend and I knew that I had to treat them the way I would want to be treated.

I wiped my face and looked at Lori and she was all dressed up for a party. I told her I was just about to take a bath. She said, great. Hurry up and put on something fresh and funky…you're coming to this New Year's Ever party with me tonight.

After dodging her for a few days, I decided to go ahead on out with her.

Lori was the type of friend where if you didn't volunteer information to her, she didn't ask. She would always ask me if I was okay, whenever she felt I was going through something but she would never ask me in depth about the situation.

Lori would only voice her opinion on my situation when I asked her to. Lori's been the same since we were in high school together.

No one could out beat Lori at partying. She partied hard. Sometimes she would party for two and three days straight. I don't know how she found that energy but she had it.

Moments later at the Mansion Party

We pulled up to a huge mansion. Lori was invited to her Doctor's New Year's Ever party at his house. Now the scary part about attending this doctor's party was that Lori was screwing around with the doctor and he happened to be a married man.

Boy, Lori always knew just how to pick them. She didn't mind being the home wrecker.

I couldn't believe I was going to the doctor's party especially not knowing if his wife was there or not.

Lori said not to worry because even if she was there, she would be so stoned she wouldn't know if she was coming or going her own damn self.

I just said forget it. Hell, it wasn't the first time I've been in a situation like this with her before and I doubt if it was the last time. But I was still just a little nervous about it.

Lori and I are older. It was time to cut some things out. I know we used to be wild and off the chain but I had a man who I loved and I wanted a family. I didn't have time for nonsense like kids.

But she assured me I had nothing to worry about.

We hopped out of the car and went inside of the house where everybody was celebrating and some folks had on their New Year's Eve party hats.

Although I was there at this party to enjoy myself, my mind was strictly on my man back at the hospital. I couldn't help but to wonder what if he woke up and I wasn't there.

I realized that I would wonder that every time I think about him and getting a little fresh air was good for me.

Lori confirmed that the doctor's wife was out of town so she asked me to go upstairs with her so that I could meet her doctor friend.

I met Dr. Sullivan, but I wasn't impressed. He asked me to make myself comfortable. I didn't know how much more comfortable I could get in a strange place.

Although his house was very nice and over the top all I could think about was the fact of him cheating with my friend and how I would feel if my man was to do that to me.

Another thing, as he greeted me with a kiss I smelled his breath. It smelled like cow waste and I tried to wipe the scent off of my jaw.

I wondered how Lori could deal with that funky breath. His breathe along would turn me off.

I made sure that I wouldn't be close enough to him to smell his breath again.

Dr. Sullivan was one of those freaky doctors to. He was very fresh with his mouth. Lori didn't care; she knew he has a thing for younger hot babes. She knew what she was doing.

He asked Lori if all of her friends were as stunning as me. Lori said, *"I would hope so."* He then asked me if I would like to party with them. I told him that I wanted to stay focused that night. He tried to get me to party by saying that a little bit won't help.

If I say no to drugs once and someone keep asking me to do it, I get irritated with them and usually I would leave. But I rode with Lori that night so as the old saying goes...I was stuck like Chuck.

What I did do was go to the restroom. Just to get away from the millionaire doctor and his freakiness.

When I got away from the doctor, I thought that I could have a breather moment. But the restroom was just as bad. Two girls were inside of the restroom making out with each other.

They looked at me and I looked back at them I guess they wanted me to leave and let them do their thing but that house had plenty bedrooms I walked pass where they could've gotten their freak on.

Finally, after seeing that I was fixing myself up in the mirror, the two women fixed their clothes and rolled their eyes at me.

Back in my days, I would have slapped a broad silly. Where I'm from you strike first because if you strike last you might not have survived.

I looked at myself in the mirror and turned away. I didn't like what I was looking at in the mirror. I didn't like me. I was angry with me.

I started to reminisce about being with my ex man whom I was still married to name Soccy.

Reminiscing Soccy house

One night while I was home with Soccy. This was before he and I was married. He threw a big New Year's Ever Party.

It was me, Soccy, his friend Rebel, and a few more of Soccy friends at our place at the time. Soccy would always sit around with his gun and drugs would be on the table for anyone who wanted to get high.

Soccy was always serious and I can't remember a time when he ever smiled. Even when he clowned around he would never crack a smile. I should have known then, that fool was crazy.

A friend of Soccy's was there from Michigan name Will. They were all getting high. Soccy smoked herbs like smoke comes from a chimney on a cold winter day.

Somehow, something went totally left field and I heard Rebel asked Soccy did he want him to throw his friend Will from Michigan out. Soccy liked his friend so he didn't allow Rebel to toss his friend out. Mainly because he knew that Will was at his maximum high. However, Will was a shyster.

I heard Will say to Soccy that he would give him his money when he damn well pleases.

I stopped drinking my drink because I knew that it would have been a matter of minutes before that guy was handled.

Soccy was trying to be cool with Will by asking him to chill and calm his voice down a bit while in his house.

Everything Soccy said to Will he took it defensively and cursed Soccy.

The next time it was Rebel telling Will to chill in his man's house.

I guess Will felt like giving it to Soccy and Rebel that night. He told Soccy that he thought he was the big man but without him he would be still riding around in a hoopty. Then, I heard Will call Soccy a Bitch!

Disrespecting Soccy in his house was the drawing point Soccy never played around with disrespect. Soccy even told Will that he was trying to be on his side but he was to respect him in his house. He told Will, must he say that to him again that there would be a problem.

Will jumped up and grabbed Soccy around his neck and choked him. The two of them started tussling. Will grabbed his gun and shot Soccy in the stomach.

Then Will started apologizing with the gun still in his hand. Soccy grabbed his gun off the table and shot back at Will but killing him instantly.

All I saw was blood everywhere and loud screaming was coming from the house. I have heard many gunshots before but I never been so close up on a person to witness them being shot.

That night and that moment was bad because Will died on the spot. I hate to revisit that moment but that night of the Doctors New Year's Eve party took me there to remember al of that horrible stuff.

When I looked back up in the mirror, I felt weak from reminiscing. So I left the out of the restroom and went back into the room where the doctor and Lori was.

As soon as I got back in the doctor's presence, he said, wow, you're back. I walked back over to the doctor and looked him in the eye and he gave me the drug to take. And I took it.

My good girl had gone out the window and the bad girl had then arrived. My mind started reminiscing a lot of things then.

Reminiscing Soccy being home from prison

I remember going to his house right after he was released from prison. He kept asking around for me and I didn't want him to know I had someone else because he would have come to get me.

So finally, I decided to meet him at his place alone. Like always, nothing could get past Soccy. He had already known about my man.

I wondered why he didn't come after me since he knew already that I was living with another man.

Soccy said that he had me fixed the moment we married. He said, that I needed to learn a thing or two about Jamaicans before I ran off and married one.

I told him that I was confused and didn't understand what he was saying to me. He said not to worry because I would find out soon. I knew he was angry with me because after he went off to prison, I never stepped a foot inside to see him at all.

He knew it was over between us. When I asked him to sign the divorce papers, he said no. He wasn't going to make it so easy for me.

I begged Soccy to sign the divorce paper but he wouldn't give in. I know he mentioned to me before that Jamaicans don't divorce. They live by the code... to death do us part.

I did do him wrong because he took care of my every need and when he went to prison, I spent over a hundred thousand dollars of his money he left me.

Well, what's done is done and we couldn't take away what was done in the past.

Soccy looked at me, then he asked me if my new man had any idea that I was still legally married to him.

I never answered the question but I did offer myself to him in exchange that he would sign the divorce papers.

I stooped so low as to bribe Soccy and to think that I could get away with offering sex to him. I figure he would a least fall for it because he was in prison for two years but he didn't.

Soccy said that I would feel the pain one day. That same pain that he felt for the last two years but mine would be worse.

I asked him was he trying to curse me, he answered and said, I cursed myself, the moment I said I do and step outside of our marriage. Then he said, *"you might not like it but, you're still my wife"*.

Soccy grabbed me hard and then faced me toward the wall and held me by my waist.

Then he told me that the old him would have screwed me as hard as he could but he won't give me the pleasure. He said he would sign the papers after my man find out that we were still bind in a contract together. He asked me to leave his place. Basically, he threw me out of his place.

I didn't know what to do from that point on. I knew that somehow I had to get out of the marriage from him before my man would have found out that I was married. The craziest thing was, I wished him gone.

I had never wished someone disappeared in my life. I realized that I had no feelings for Soccy at all to think like that. He gave me all the reasons to feel that way. He was such a cheat anyways. He couldn't keep his penis in his pants if you paid him to before he went to prison. But he had the nerves to turn me down.

No I didn't feel sorry about wishing he would disappear. All he did was bring me sorrow and pain in the relationship.

All I thought about was my man, and how he would feel believing in me then to find out that I was never truthful with him. Not only was I dishonest but also the worse of it was, I was a married woman. Not to the man I loved. I was married to a man I never was in love with.

All the way to my man place, all I thought about was my deception to him after I left Soccy's house.

When I made it home, my man asked me where had I been. I told my man I was visiting an old friend. My man asked me if he knew this old friend and offered me some dinner.

I told him no and that the old friend wasn't that important and yes, I would love to have something to eat.

Knowing I wasn't hungry, I ate with him just to keep his mind off of questioning me. Although the food smelled delicious I just wasn't in it.

He did notice I was uptight. So he poured me and glass of wine and fixed me a plate and we sat down and ate dinner together.

I didn't like the direction I was headed in. It was a dark area and that wasn't a good feeling. But still, I didn't know how to come clean with my man. I just wanted that deep secret go away somehow. Nothing just goes away until you make it go away. That night, all I wanted to do after dinner was lie down and sleep. So I did.

Then, the next morning I got up and I still wasn't myself. My man was on his way to work and I carried on with the morning as I usually do. I would make coffee in the mornings and have a slice of toast and juice. But that particular morning I burned the toast.

My man scared me when he came up behind me because I didn't hear him coming. So I jumped and he asked me if I was okay. I told him yes. But really I was still thinking about ways to get Soccy to sign the divorce papers or a way out of the divorce.

My man told me that I seemed to be a little troubled since that day before and I denied it. He asked me if I still loved him and I told him with all my heart.

Told me to take it easy that morning. I was going to try and clear my head before it was time to meet my man for lunch that afternoon.

I wanted my man to understand that me quitting the job had nothing to do with how I had been feeling lately. Even though I went to school for Broadcast TV and I worked at an advertising agency as an administrative assistant.

I told him that I Had some issues that I needed to straighten out with my sisters. And there was another lie. I hate to tell lies because lies are never ending. When you tell one lie you have to tell another one and after so many lies, you forget the original lie. You can't win for loosing with lies, I tell ya.

After he kissed me I told him that I would see him in a few hours. I was so happy to be with my man but I wasn't happy with myself. I couldn't even call my sisters because they had no clue I was even married to Soccy. They hated his guts anyway.

So I called Lori and she never answered. Then my phone rung back and it was Soccy asking me if I would meet him for lunch. He said he was willing to sign the divorce papers.

A part of me wondered if he was for real or just playing games with me. However, it was worth taking the chance so I decided to meet up with him. But not at his place. I asked him if we could meet some place downtown.

I needed to be in the public eye to meet Soccy. This man served time in prison for murder and I didn't want him to be so pissed off with me that I would be his next victim.

So we decided to meet up at the café we would eat at all the time when we were together a few years back.

I arrived at the café first. I must have sat there a good thirty minutes before Soccy came. I was willing to wait on him. All I thought about was Soccy signing those divorce papers. I could have been my old self and had someone else to sign them but I didn't want anything to come back to bite me in the ass when my life would be looking up with my man now.

I looked at the time and it was already thirty five minute I had been waiting on Soccy. It took me back to the time when Soccy and I first got married.

Reminiscing marriage to Soccy

Never happily married but we got married because we were both high and drunk at the time and fooling around in Vegas we were just doing something.

By the time we had gotten married, it was too late to bail out and we tried to make it work as a married couple.

Soccy was sitting at the table and I went to get my little sister Megan from the front door. She was looking to see what table we were sitting at. Soccy Jamaican friend name Rebel was having lunch with us also.

When I made it back to the table I introduced my sister to Soccy and Rebel. My sister was calm at first at meeting Soccy and Rebel. She talked about how hungry she was and why we had to sit in the back where she couldn't spot us. I told Megan to relax. Then Soccy told her she needed to take a chill pill. So Megan looked at me and said, *"tell me they just yo friends and you ain't dating neither one of them, right"*. Soccy jumped in the conversation and said; *he ma…what you mean by that. What we look like to you?* Megan looked at them and said; *"some fools, with ya hair all twisted up"*.

Rebel asked me if she was my real sister or what. Megan told me that if I had invited her to meet Soccy and Rebel, she could have went to get her feet massage.

Rebel told her that he would message her feet. Megan declined the offer. Soccy looked at Megan and said, *"why don't you just tell sweet little sis, that were married and she has a new brother-in-law"* Megan looked at me and asked what was he talking about.

I told Megan we got married in Vegas last week. Megan looked at me and said, *"Really, does Angie know about this. So you're married to a Jamaican, a dreadlock. You know how controlling them Jamaicans are. Next thing you know he'll be trying to whip you butt!"*

Soccy asked Megan, *why is it that she referred to him as a Jamaican and not call him by his name.* Megan ignored him as if he wasn't talking.

I told Megan that Angie knew as of that morning also and didn't have anything negative to say. She said she wasn't being negative she was just giving me the facts and that no penis was that good.

Soccy asked her how did she know if no penis was that good if she never had a good penis.

I had to stop the conversation between Soccy and my sister Megan because things would have escalated way out control.

Megan jumped and told me she was going to leave because she did not want any Voodoo Jamaican Hex stuff lingering on her. Soccy told Megan it was nice meeting her to and he was glad to be a part of the family.

I asked Megan not to leave but she wasn't hearing it. Soccy said that he was happy to get off to a good start with my sister. He said she was just like me, had a fiery attitude. Soccy said that Jamaica they call it truculent.

By then I was hearing Soccy voice at the restaurant where we were met me to sign the divorce papers.

I heard Soccy voice saying, *"Aw, so you're daydreaming."* I told him I was sitting there for nearly an hour waiting for him and that I had some place to be shortly.

Soccy didn't have much conversation for me. The first thing he asked me for was the divorce documents. I handed him the divorce papers and told him where he should sign and he signed them with no problems.

After Soccy signed the papers, he handed it back to me. He told me to have a good life. I told him to do the same.

I was so relieved and it was like a big heavy weight lifted off of me. Now I just have to get through the divorce process without my man finding out that I was even married.

I found myself waking up from reminiscing that moment.

CHAPTER 5

CHURCH DAY

VICTORY church of CHRIST

The next morning I woke up in my bed from the New Years Ever Party that Lori had invited me to. I had a slight hang over but didn't remember much about what happened at the party at all. As I walked toward the living room Lori was in the front room reading a magazine.

Lori looked at me and said she was happy to see me up finally because I had gotten so wasted at the Doc's party last night. She just wanted to make sure that I got home safe and woke up safe.

I asked Lori what happened because I could not remember a thing. Lori laughed and little and told me that I was way to loaded to remember anything but just know I had a time of my life and my sadness had left for the moment.

I was hoping I didn't enjoy myself to much. I already had a lot to handle.

Lori had to go home and get herself together. My mind was on my man and getting back to the hospital.

My sister Angie text me to see if I was going to church. I decided to go to church anyway that New Years Day as I always do. It was more of a confirmation that I needed to be at church and not skip it to be at the hospital when I received the text. '

When I arrived at the church, I was glad to be there. At Victory Church of Christ it would usually be me and my man along with my sisters and their men attending every first Sunday of the month. I knew it would help me throughout the day to get that spiritual nourishment from God.

Although I grew up in the hood, the lady who cared for us over at the foster home kept me and my sisters in church every Sunday.

I arrived at the church just in time to hear my sister Angie lead the choir. You could hear the joyful music of the sweet choir as soon as the church door opened. The congregation danced to the gospel music.

Every first Sunday the "Victory Church of Christ" would a have a surprise guest singer. That particular Sunday happened to be John Franklin. A big time gospel artist on the music scene.

I saw Richard and I went over to where he was and sat next him. I hugged him and then my sister Megan came over to sit with us and I gave her a hug. My sister was still leading the gospel song with the choir.

Richard loves church. He sings every song and so does Megan. My sister Angie can direct a choir like I have never seen anyone do before.

She makes sure that the singers use every vocal cord they have at that church.

I love our Pastor to. He also bounces to the music just as much as the congregation.

After the praise song Pastor James took the mic and said, *"If you love the Lord let me hear you say AMEN,"* the entire congregation said *"AMEN"*. Pastor James asked the congregation to give the Lord a big round of applause and to welcome our Guest singer John Franklin. John Franklin came out to sing and it was touching to hear that man sing.

My sister Megan saw how touched I was from the song and she decided to hold on tight to me. She told me that everything was going to work itself out. I appreciate those words coming from her more so than everything and anything else, which usually would just fly from her mouth.

After church was over, Richard said they were going to have a Sunday lunch back at his house. His mother and Ante had already prepared the meals. I agreed to go over to my sister place for a little bit before I would head over to the hospital.

Sunday Brunch at Angie's house

When I got there food was already on the table and ready to eat. I told Miss Henderson that the food looked great and that I wished I knew how to cook the way she cooks.

Miss Henderson could make anything there is to make and put soul and love in it. I have never seen so much food prepared at one time.

Richard told me to stop filling his mothers head up and stop making his wife feel bad because she doesn't know how to cook.

Angie said she knows how to cook. She just don't cook much cause since Richards mother moved in, she enjoys doing the cooking much.

Cooking is a hobby for Miss Henderson and from the taste of her food I knew that she put all of her energy into it.

Megan sitting across the table hollowed out and said that was the reason why she knew fashion so well because she loved to shop. Miss Henderson agreed with her.

Richard Ante Loretta came into the dining room holding Reign, Richard and Angie's daughter. Loretta said, *"hey guys, look who's up",* Richard got up from the table and grabbed Reign. I told Angie she had gotten so big and was growing up to fast for me.

I noticed Reign has some Chanel earrings in her ear and I asked Angie who bought her Chanel earrings. Before Angie could say anything, Megan said that she was responsible for the Glam piece of Jewel. I knew Megan had bought the Chanel earrings without her saying she had bought them. Angie would never buy a two year old a pair of seven thousand dollars earrings.

Megan showed off her earrings and said that her niece Reign was a mini her. Richard looked at Megan and said "No" just like that. Megan said "YES" just like that.

It was nice to see that Megan spoiled Reign so much since she was the first one to have something to say when Angie announce she and Richard were expecting a baby.

Angie changed the subject by complimenting Miss Henderson on her Mac and Cheese Dish. Angie said it took her two years to get her body back in shape and each week she eats Mac and cheese with two thousand calories in it because Miss Henderson's Mac and Cheese was so irresistible. Miss Henderson was thrilled with all of the compliments we gave her. Afterwards she got up from the table to grab the desert. Richard ante Loretta decided to give her a hand.

Richard asked me if there were any improvement in my man condition. I told him there were no changes so far. The doctors said that it was up to my man to see if the medicine will make him strong enough to manage on to fight off the infection on his own.

Megan hates when the doctors would say anything on a person's life good or bad because she says, there not God. Only God knows what will happen.

Megan feels those doctors, goes off of scientific facts and not the work of God.

Angie knew what direction this conversation would head in so she changed the subject. Angie goes, *"hey guys, we have another surprise!*

Megan guessed Angie was going to make another announcement about being pregnant again. But it was nothing close to it.

"Let us guess… Angie's pregnant again". Angie goes, *"not yet, but we did find our mother.* Megan booed that surprise.

I asked Angie how was she able to pull that one off after so many years. Angie said with the help of Richard's good friend.

Megan wanted no part of knowing about our biological mother.

Angie and I were open to meet her and we were peculiar on wondering whom she would look like?

Megan didn't understand why we were interest in seeing someone who chose crack over there kids.

Angie told Megan that no one is perfect and we should want to talk to her to see what really happened.

It was plain and clear in Megan eyes to what happened when they were just kids.

On the positive side, I was happy that the three of us was kept together because the State could have separated us was kept together.

Angie said, *"Well, there is another thing. I found out that we have a brother"*.

Megan said that that whole situation was getting freakier by the minute. I wanted to know where was he and if he was alive and if so did he get a chance to live with our mother.

Angie told us that he was in San Diego and she was still gathering the information on him. Megan said good luck to him and as far as she knows, she never had a brother, a mother or a father.

Richard look at her and said, *"and just how do you think you came into this world Miss Megan" Megan replied, "the same way that we all did, through somebody's vagina"*.

By that time, Miss Henderson and Loretta came back to the table with two cakes and a pie.

Miss Henderson sat down and said, *"I heard everything from the kitchen. I have known you girls for ten years now and you are all lovely young women. I love each of you and I know about your foster care and I know about your biological mother had a disease.*

Megan said, *it wasn't a disease Miss Henderson, she smoked crack and took in all other type of drugs.*

Miss Henderson said, *I know. And having an addiction is a disease. We all do things when were young. It's not always about what you have done in your past, its what you're doing now to change yourself from whom you once were in the past and where you headed. As long as you're living and healthy, you can change and change sometimes doesn't come over night. Sometimes it could take a day, a month, or even years. Like I have told my son and my other children, you guys are young and have it a lot more easier, than we had it growing up. And remember some people aren't fortunate enough to get second chances. Cherish it and accept it. You got the opportunity to meet your mother, accept that great gift from God. Talk to her and find out what happened and why she chose another life over you all. I believe you will have closure on that side of your life.*

Wow, I couldn't do nothing but thank Miss Henderson for such an encouraging moment. Which took me back to my man. So I instantly asked everyone to excuse me from the table because I needed to get back to the hospital. And I thank them for such a great lunch after church.

CHAPTER 6

A TRICKY MIND

Back at the hospital

I left had left Angie and Richards house and drove back to the hospital. It had started to rain and I didn't want to walk from the parking lot to inside because I didn't have an umbrella with me. So the hospital has Valet parking. I used the valet attendant to part my car.

All I could think about was getting to my man. It's been four days since he had been hospitalized. And twenty-four hours since I left the hospital.

When I made it up to the floor of the hospital I walked pass the nurse station on the ICU floor.

When I made it to the room, I saw this beautiful woman standing over my man bed and talking to him.

Excuse me, I said to her. *Who are you*? This woman turned around with a great big smile and said that she and my man worked together years ago. Then she introduced herself as "Halle Robinson". Then she asked me my name and I told her my name. Vivian Carter.

She said that she and Tie go way back. I asked her who was Tie.

She said, never mind her, she just started calling him Tie after he was so crazy about a black neck tie she bought him for Christmas one year.

I said. "Oh really". He's never mentioned you before. She said oh, Tie was just modest like that and very private.

I wanted to know how long had she known about my man being there in the hospital.

She tried to convince me that although Tie was in Chicago and she was in New York, that they never lost communication.

Then she went on to say the only reason they weren't together is because she took a job in New York and Tie didn't want to lose.

Said oh, she and my man never lost communication. She just moved to New York to take a job there as an Anchor Woman and Tie didn't want to relocate. She also said after she didn't hear from him for a few days that she called his mother and asked where he was. His mother told her that she was in the hospital and she took a flight as soon as possible to get to him.

She looked at me and said that Tie had been in the hospital on numerous of occasions but never as bad as to put him on a breathing machine.

She said that normally when Tie get sick, he would come home after a day or two. But it scares her to know that he was in an induced coma.   Halle asked me what my name was again.

I said, Vivian.   Then she called me Viv!   This woman went on to tell me about the first time she and Tie met was at the Metra Station around the time she was studying at DePaul University.   I had to interrupt her.

I said. *"Look, Halle, if you don't mind to excuse yourself, he's my man now"*.

Halle looked at my man then looked back at me and said, *"Oh, oh silly me. Why I didn't have a clue. I mean, no one told me anything of such.*

I didn't care what she had to say from that point on, I just knew she had to leave and out of respect for my man, I asked her nicely to get the hell out of my man hospital room and when my man awake I might think about telling him that she had come to visit him.

This strange woman who I had never heard my man talk about a day in his life left.   I walked over close to my man bed and watched him as he slept.   The nurse came in and spoke and started changing my man IV. While she was doing so I couldn't help but to wonder who that strange woman was. So I asked the nurse if she had seen that woman before. Did she come in yesterday while I was away?

The nurse said, what woman. I said the woman who just left as you were coming in. The nurse apologized and said she never saw any woman leave. And no one besides me had been there all day.

I ask her if she was sure and the nurse assured me that no one had come in to see my man and neither did anyone leave the room just now.

I looked at my watch and the time. I noticed my watch said it was eight o'clock pm. I asked the nurse what time it was and she confirmed it was eight o'clock pm.

I tried to figure out how could that possibly be when I made it hear it was around two pm.

The nurse told me that when she came in on her shift at three pm that I was standing in the same place. She said she had been outside at the nurse station the whole time and that I had been there just as long as she have.

The nurse asked me if I was okay. I told her I was fine. That I had lost track of time and nothing else. I must have been daydreaming to lose track of time like that. I felt really tired.

I pulled up a chair close to my man bed and sat there throughout the night.

The next morning I woke up freezing cold from sleeping in the chair all night. I realized that for three days, I never saw any sunshine. Not even throughout the day.

When I looked over at my man, I heard a big voice saying hello. I looked over and it was Uncle John.

Uncle John would always bring joy to any life. He would always call me Sugar. Uncle John came over and gave me a hug and a big kiss. He was so loud or maybe he just seemed to be loud because I had just awake.

He said that Joanne gave him the information and he stopped through there to see his favorite Nephew.

Uncle John looked over at my man and said, *"Whoa, nephew, what the hell they got in ya here".* *He ain't looking to pretty right now. When you get well we gone have some beers and go duck hunting!'*

Then Uncle John looked over at me and said, *"when that boy was weigh little I would take him Duck hunting and one time he light a been shot my foot off… ain't lying, ask his momma. She would hate when I would take him in up in them woods and hunt fa them ducks. Then, we would take em', skin em' and put on the fire! "*

Uncle John looked over at me and asked me how I've been holding up these past few days.

I told him that it's been rough but each day I'm hoping my man would awake.

Uncle John said that I didn't look so good. Maybe I should try not to worry. I told Uncle

John that I hadn't slept well the past few days and I had been at the hospital most of the time.

Uncle John said that he ain't slept well all his life. But he know his nephew gone pull through.

Then he said, "Well sugar, Uncle John gone head on back foe I can get to fishing! When my nephew wake up and get well we gone go fishing fa some of those cat fish. We use to deep-fry some catfish to. Nephew would catch cat fish bigger than him when he was a knee high. We would skin them to. Take em' and cut they guts out and deep-fry them till the meal got golden brown and crispy.

Put some of that Louisiana hot sauce and eat it to the fish bone. You had the deep fried southern cat fish sugar. You know what I'm talking bout don't ya?

I said, *"yes sir I have.'* Uncle John said, *"well you gone have some mo. Nephew will be awake and here soon."*

Uncle John told me to take care and he will see us soon. He walked out of the room and started singing Otis Redman song.

When Uncle John left the room. I went into the restroom to use to toilet. After I flush the toilet, I heard a woman talking to my man. When I peeked out it was my man Grand Ma Rose at his bedside.

I had to scratch my head because either I was going crazy or I was dreaming. So I closed the restroom door and ran water to wash my face. Then the voice stopped.

I told myself that maybe I was sleep walking. I laughed at myself and looked at the time and it was still early morning.

I opened the door and saw Grand Ma Rose at his bedside. Telling my man to fight. Grand Ma Rose didn't even notice me. I even called her name a few times and she never heard me call her name. I was going to touch Grand Ma Rose but then she said not to touch her because her body was to cold. Then Grand Ma Rose carried on talking to my man.

I knew then that I was dreaming. Grand Ma Rose said, *"sleep son, you need to rest because we got a big day ahead of us tomorrow."*

I said, *Grand Ma Rose, you're not real. You died five years ago.* Grand Ma Rose never responded to me. Then I heard her say, *"You know your Uncle John passed away from a heart disease a year ago and all he talked about was how much he missed you before he passed. Yo momma knew how much you loved yo Uncle and she didn't want you to worry son. When I first found out you were sick I told her then not to worry that you will have a long life. I love you son. But you gone be all right. Just don't give up. It ain't yo time yet. You got plenty of time left. That's right. Plenty of time."*

Then Grand Ma Rose look at me and said, *"you can go on home dear and stop worrying yo little heart out. He'll be home soon. He's gone need your strength."*

Then Grand Ma Rose walked out of the room and walk out. I looked down at the time and the clock was still moving. So why can't I wake up. I want to wake up.

I called out Grand ma Rose name and went to the door and I didn't see her walking down the hall at all. As a matter of fact I didn't see not a nurse in sight. So I told myself that I was dreaming.

I kept screaming hello for the nurse but no one heard me. So I started walking down the hallway and I saw all of the other sick patients in their room as if everything was normal.

Still I didn't see a nurse in sight. Then finally at the end of the hallway, I saw a nurse and I was relieved to see the nurse. I asked her if she could help me.

I told her I was dreaming and I couldn't wake up from the dream and I want to because my man was alone and something isn't right. The nurse said she would be right there to help me in a minute.

It was really weird because when I walked back to the room my sister Megan was there beside my man bed talking to him. When she saw me enter the room she said, *"there you are sis, I've been looking for you."*

I looked at Megan and looked out of the door and everything was back to normal. The nurses were all at their station. One of the nurses even looked up at me as if I was disturbed.

I said, *"Megan, when did you get here?" The* first thing Megan said to me was "Happy New Year my beautiful sister. I knew you would be here. Angie and I tried calling you all night but you never answered.

I asked her how long had she been in the room and she told me she had been there for a least 20 minutes and the nurse told her that I had stepped out for a minute.

Then I asked Megan, if I had just come through the door. Megan dropped her head and said, *"Are you kidding me"; no you came through the window. What's that all about? You probably need to sleep and leave this hospital honey. I just came by to check on my brother-in-law and you".*

I told Megan that I saw Grand Ma Rose, my man grandmother in here standing next to my man bed and talking to him. Megan looked around the room and said, *"Really, now I know you're missing sleep. That old hag has been dead over five years now. I mean, no disrespect but you're starting to talk real creepy now. I think its time to go. Now you see why I tell you about soul tying with them Voo Doo Jamaican's and You know how I feel about spiritual stuff, I don't trust Haitians, Jamaican's, Africans, them folks from the Island, , hell, I don't even trust our government, nor them Dirty South Boys from Louisiana. But, I love me some Little Wayne though, he is from Louisiana ain't he?"*

My energy was so low all I could say to my sister was, *"yeah"*.

Megan then said, *"Little Wayne can throw all kinds of hex my way as long as the Chanel and Gucci's are part of the whole Hex deal."*

After her whole ordeal with Little Wayne, Megan told me that she loved me and asked me to go home, get some sleep and get away from the hospital for a while. Well, that's much easier to say than to do.

CHAPTER 7

THE ESTATE

Taking a break to myself

I left the hospital and went up the street to have a cup of soup. I was watching the news and looking around and people were laughing and enjoying life.

Life was not good for me for those three days. I smiled when I saw a little old couple walk in the café together. They were so cute together. I wondered if my man and I will have the chance to grow old together and still love each other the same. I miss him so much.

The waitress came up to me and asked me if there was anything else she could get for me. I couldn't really eat anything.

When she brought me the check, I looked at it and paid the bill. I only paid enough to cover the bill. Although I was tired, I wasn't to tired to tip. So I left the money on the table with the check.

By the time I got outside, I thought about it and turned around. I decided from that moment on, I wanted do people right and change my heart on things.

So I went back inside of the Café and left the waitress a twenty dollar tip. She was really happy to receive that tip.

I started smiling because I felt good to tip someone out of ten years. Ten years, I had never ever tipped no one.

I went home to shower. After the shower, I took my bike out for a bike ride. It felt good to ride my bike. The sun still wasn't shining but that was okay. I was enjoying the bike ride like never before.

After the bike ride, I made it back home and started cleaning up the place.

While I was cleaning, the phone ranged. It was Lori asking me to meet her at her Ante Ruth's Jazz club.

It had been a while since I had listened to Aunt Ruth sing at her own club. Usually she's singing around the world.

Aunt Ruth's Jazz Club

Lori and I were sitting at a reserved table. Aunt Ruth was beautiful in her dazzling evening gown. The way her voice flow reminds me of spring water you can drink from a flowing river.

The sweet sound of Jazz from Aunt Ruth touched my heart. Out of all the days this was the first day I had gone through where I did not reminisce about my man. Although, my man was on my mind. I just felt the need to take care of me and get back to being and feeling beautiful.

Lori rubbed me on my shoulder. Then Lori cousin Nick came to the table with a friend of his name Keven. I had already met Nick before a few times. He said it was nice to see me again and introduced me to his friend Keven.

Boy Nick sure was handsome, but he's like family. Keven, on the other hand, who I had never met before was even more handsome.

Keven asked if we were enjoying the show and I told him the show had just started. Lori looked at me and smiled.

Keven looked at me and said, *"Wow, you are beautiful."* I just simply smiled at him and started listening to Aunt Ruth as she sang her next song.

Nick and Lori got up to dance. Keven asked me if he could have a dance with me.

I thought, why the hell not. So I said, *"Lets do it."*

Keven and I got up to slow dance and he asked me why haven't we met before. Well I couldn't answer that question. But I did say that people usually meet at the right time in their life.

Keven didn't doubt it but he said, he knew it was impossible for me to be single.

I shared with him the fact that I had a man who was at the hospital fighting for his life and whom I happened to love very much.

Keven said he was sorry to hear my story and I told him that sorry does nothing for my mind and I, so he didn't have to be sorry. I was just blessed that my man was still alive.

I even told Keven about how I had spent the last three days waiting by my man bedside for him to awake until I finally decided to get out and get some fresh air.

Aunt Ruth song ended right as I told him not to be sorry. Everyone stopped dancing and applauded Aunt Ruth for such a remarkable song.

I was glad to have that dance with Keven. Not that I was interested in him but it felt good to dance.

At the end of the night Keven and Nick walked Lori and I to the car to make sure we got to the car safe.

Keven asked me if he could give me his number just in case I would like to talk sometimes. I took his number because I saw no harm in taking his number. He seemed like a real gentlemen.

Nick told us to be safe and told Lori to call him once she made it home. Lori told him she was staying with me tonight.

After Lori pulled off from the club, she asked me what did I think of Keven. I told her that he seemed to be a nice man and very handsome and tall. She said that all of her cousin friends were tall because most of them are his NBA buddy's.

I wanted to know Keven's story because he did look a little familiar. That's when I learned I had seen him talking on the sports channel as a sport announcer on game days.

CHAPTER 8

SEARCHING FOR UNDERSTANDING

Back at the hospital, the next day.

It was the next morning. I was on my way to the hospital to see my man. I stopped by the flower shop downstairs from the hospital to put some fresh flowers in his room.

When I walked in his room, I was caught by surprise from that same woman name Halle. She happened to be there in my man room again, wearing the same clothes she wore yesterday.

I said, "umm why are you here again?" She replied. *Because I have a right to be here. I should be asking you that question. You see, I only gave you time to see Tie because you seemed to be very week over him. It's obvious. I figured there was someone else because although I talked to him, we didn't see each other for months at a time.*

I told this woman she needed to leave or I would call security to get her thrown out. She said don't bother, that I would be thrown out before she would. Then she said, *"you know Viv, I didn't come here because I want your man, I came here because I need to know about all of his Estate just incase, he does die. Therefore, I have been meeting with my attorneys to get some things settled between me and my estranged husband."*

I said, *"yo what"*. Halle replied, *"oh you didn't know. He never told you that he and I never legally divorced. So sad you had to find out this way."*

Then she went on to say that later on my man had tried to divorce her numerous of times but she would fight it because she knew he was sick and she had to get what she deserved from the marriage.

I said how sick! Halle said, no not as sick as Tie is over there.

I told her to show me proof she was ever married to my man. She pulled out her marriage certificate to prove to me she and my man were married.

I told her it could be a fake. She said if I did not believe her I could just run on down to cook county court house and pull up the marriage License myself.

I told her I did not believe her. She said, I didn't have to believe her. But what I had to do was be nice to her because being nice would get me the answers I needed.

I had no clue to what that lady was saying to me. Then she went on to tell me that if I wasn't nice to her that she would reverse the slipper and have me banned from entering my man hospital room.

She gave me big attitude and then left the room.

Well, I must have been dreaming again because I woke up sitting next to my man by his bedside and realized that I was dreaming again. This time the nurse woke me up and asked me if I knew someone by the name of Halle and if so, she was waiting downstairs to come up.

The nurse said that if this person is close family like she said she was, her name should be on the close family list.

At first, I said no, then I asked the nurse to have her to come up. The nurse said that she would call down to the front desk lobby and have her to come up.

I turned around to look at my man. Then I went to the restroom to powder up a little.

I stepped out from the restroom and Halle came inside and knocked at the door. Asking me if it was alright if she came in. She had a total different attitude. It didn't seem like the same lady I dreamt about. But she was as real as my dream was to see her in the flesh. I told her to come on in.

Then she introduced herself. I told her that I knew who she was already. She smiled and said that she was surprised that my man ever even talked about her.

Then she looked over at my man to say it was two years since she had heard from my man. He had been on her mind and when she called Joanne after she couldn't reach him a few times, she learned that he was in the hospital fighting for his life.

She gave me this weird look and said my man would talk about me all of the time. He loves you so much.

I told her that I knew that. Cutting her off from speaking, I got straight to it and asked her if she and my man were ever married and if there was something between then two that I should know have known about.

Halle seemed to be very surprised of me asking her that so she said, *"married, oh gosh no. I was his therapist for five years.*

I had this look of confusion and that woman saw it all up in me. She asked me if I'd like to take a walk with her.

I thought boy, at that time it was a good idea for me to take a long walk so I could figure out what the hell was going on with me. I was losing my mind or I'm dreaming of some real negative things.

As we walked and talked outside of the hospital, I realized that I was having a crisis moment there. It happens mostly when I was inside of my man hospital room.

Halle asked me to take a deep breath and I did so. Then she said, from her experience, that it seemed to her as if I was having a heraldry moment. I said, *"a what, I'm not crazy lady?"*

Halle went on to say well, sometimes the mind can be tricky and a heraldry meaning, You're dreaming of stories within a story. It is the allusion of a person placing an image of a small shield on top of a larger shield.

She told me that I was creating my own dreams for me to have dreamt I was seeing his deceased grandmother and uncle and even, placing herself, in the image. Halle then went on to say that my dreams, seems to go further than that as if my dreams had a deeper root.

So I asked Halle to explain to me how I had dreamt of her because my man had never mentioned her name before ever.

Halle was so sure that my man must have mentioned her somehow in order for me to place an image of her in my dreams.

Halle said that if I was to talk to my man, that he would hear me. He just can't respond. Halle said that although my man loved me, he battled with his inner spirit mainly for after he took another man's life.

Halle told me that my man was always concerned with how the burglar parents must have felt and he never got the change to ask for forgiveness because the police force did not allow him to come in close contact with the suspect family.

I said to her, Halle, my man was the best thing that ever happened to me. I also told her that I did not want to continue the dreams. I asked her for advice so that I wouldn't have dreams like that anymore.

She told me I could start by going to visit my man by his bedside.

Did this woman just hear anything I just said to her and where in the world did she come from?

So I asked her goofy voice but if she had heard the things I was saying to her. Because the way she started talking was confusing me even more.

Halle said yes, this is why we met here. I said, no, no, no we met a short while ago upstairs and you asked me to take a walk remember.

Halle had such a serious look on face and said, *no you invited me in. You invited me hear. You called me up and said that your man was in the hospital and you knew about me because your man had talked about me a few times from being his therapist. You told me you got my number from his wallet at home. Are you saying you don't remember any of this? Vivian, I haven't stepped foot in that hospital yet. Halle looked at me and said, that I needed to really take some time out for me.*

She tried to make me believe that I introduced myself to her when I called her to talk to her about coming in town and I arranged for her to fly in.

But if this all was true, why did she call Joanne. She had an answer for that to. Supposedly, she called Joanne after we talked.

I called her a liar and devil. She did say I had invited her in and the devil just doesn't come in unless you invite it. So I told her I made a mistake to invite her in.

I offended her but I didn't care. How is it she tried to make me seem crazy and out of my mind, telling me that I was creating some image of an illusion or whatever.

She said she would not stand to accept any verbal abuse from no one. Then she pulled out a card and wrote a number on the back of it and said that maybe she would come back to see my man.

Before she left my presence she advised me that it would be in my best interest to contact that number on the back of her card for some help from a good friend who would be willing to help me.

The only help I needed was for my man to wake up from that whole coma mess. Then I wouldn't have had all those issues or seeing dead folks and seeing that woman with the daffy duck voice. WTF!

Then she went on to say that there was nothing I could do for my man but pray and ask God to watch over him and wait until his body is ready to function on its own to live life again and not to live a life of sorrow because sorry will cause a meltdown eventually.

I said lady, Halle or whatever your name is, please if you're leaving just go, and she left.

Back upstairs inside of the hospital

I ran upstairs to see my man. I saw the nurse in my man room changing his IV.

I said, *excuse me*. The nurse answered, *yes*. I said, *umm, didn't you just change that out*. The nurse said *no, this is the first time since four am that his IV was changed.*

Then the nurse went on to say, *that it was good to see a love one here for him. No one has visited him since we first brought him in three days ago. A few of the nurses took days on bringing him fresh flowers each day.*

I glanced over at the flowers on the desk and noticed they were different then the flowers I brought that afternoon.

Then as the nurse was leaving out, *she looked at me and asked me if I was feeling okay.*

I told her that I was just fine. Then the nurse said that I looked like I had just seen a ghost.

I left the hospital and went to grab some coffee. I was still thinking about all of that madness. I was feeling a little upset just because.

In the process I was wondering and thinking, I must be still dreaming because I know I have been at that hospital everyday all day and I only miss one half of a day not being her on New Years Eve.

I started to wonder if something was wrong with me because I pinch myself and it hurt. So I couldn't have been dreaming.

As I was preparing to leave, I asked the cashier what was the date and she said it was New Year's Day, January 1st.

No it can't be. New Year's Day has already passed. I was in church on New Year's Day. I had brunch at Angie and Richard's house on New Year's Day. All of those thoughts were cramping my head.

So then I asked her what time was it and she told me it was nine am in the morning.

Then I asked her to tell me the day of the week. She said it was Sunday morning, the first Sunday of the month.

Then I received a text from Angie asking if I was going to church that day for first Sunday. I thought maybe that was the text from her yesterday but the text just came in

 I thought that maybe my sisters text was a re text. Sometimes my text sends out twice. So I walked toward the restroom to wash my hands and why were all of the customers staring at me. They all starred at me and I starting hearing everybody's conversation all though they were talking quietly.

My ears were massively in pain. I covered my ears until I got to inside of the restroom.

I looked in the mirror and when I looked at my clothes, it was the same outfit I saw myself with at church yesterday. But how could that be when I was in church yesterday and we always go on New Year's Day.

Then I thought, maybe I put the same church clothes on this morning. Maybe the waitress said it was Monday and not Sunday. Yeah, that's what she said, it was Monday, the first Monday of the month.

I walked out of the restroom and there wasn't a customer in sight. I asked the waitress where did everyone go.

The waitress assumed they had all left because the coffee shop was closing. She asked me if I was okay because I was in the restroom for quite some time.

Then she asked me if there was anything else she could get for me because they were closing in in ten minutes and she likes to get home before ten pm to watch nightly news.

I looked out of the coffee shop window and it was dark already.

I took out my compact mirror from my purse to look at myself and realized, I had on a different outfit other than the church outfit I had worn on New Year's Day for church.

Then I heard the bell from twinkling to alert the servers on when customers come thru the coffee shop.

I heard Keven voice say to me, yes you are beautiful. I turned around and he was standing behind me with a big smile.

He asked how I was doing and I said that it was rough for me but I was going to make it.

Keven said he was trying to catch a cup of hot coffee in just the Nick of Time before the coffee shop closed.

I looked at Keven and he had the same outfit on from last night at the Jazz Club.

He was talking to me but I didn't know a word he was saying because my mind was totally in bliss by now. I had to shake myself out back into what he was saying. I was so sick of people asking me if I was okay. I must have had the word sympathy written all over my face.

So I did hear him say that he had just left his attorney's office and decided to grab a hot cup of coffee on the way home. He said it was a surprise to see me and I was looking just as lovely as I did yesterday.

I said oh good. I'm so glad to know it was yesterday.

Keven ask me to come again and I had to explain it where he didn't know I was going through some things I simply could not explain.

So I said yes, I'm so glad I met you yesterday.

I did play it off well because I said that I was having a slight headache and if it was possible I would love to talk with him later.

Keven was content with that. He said it was nice seeing me again and asked me if I would be interested in going to see Jack Miller play as Ludwig van Beethoven at the Opera House Friday night.

I barely knew what day it was and the rate I was going how would I know Friday night from Saturday night to Tuesday night.

Then he felt selfish and said he apologized for his manners. There was no need to apologize. I was the one confused with the days so I just asked him if he could give me a few days just to think about it.

He didn't pressure me in to a sure answer and I liked that.

I thought that dream was over, but I was still dreaming because what happened next was crazy.

There I was sleeping at the coffee table as if I hadn't slept in days. The next thing I knew, I was falling out of the chair and onto the floor.

I must have been sleeping on my elbow because once it slipped off the coffee table, that's how I lost my balance and ended up on the floor.

Again, I was dreaming this whole time I was sitting there in the coffee house. I was so glad to wake up. Everyone starred at me.

The cashier came over to help wipe up the spilled coffee. She said that she tried to wake me up but she could tell I needed the rest. Then she asked me if that was Kevin DuWall, the basketball star that I was talking to when I first came in.

She already knew it was Kevin DuWall. I don't know why some people go so far to ask you questions they already know.

I said uh huh, but what happened. It was just night. I thought the shop was closed. But I had to say to myself, get used to the dreams until I can find out what was going on with me. Act normal otherwise people will think that I was losing my mind.

I looked through my cell phone and didn't see a single text from Angie.

Then waitress was still going on about how she loved Keven and was a big fan when he played for the Wizards and he was so fine. Then she said, oops, I'm sorry. That ain't yo man is he? I asked her if that day was Monday and she said yes. I said thanks and no, he's not my man. My man is in the hospital sick. Then the waitress said, oh...okay and I left the coffee house.

Back at home listening to music.

The next thing I knew I was playing some Beethoven musical then I poured a glass of wine and sat on the couch. When I woke up I heard an alarm go off and it was the next morning.

CHAPTER 9

LEARNING TO FORGIVE

Later that day

That morning seemed normal for me. I was getting dressed to meet my sisters and my biological mother. We all met up at our favorite spots, the Bahama Breeze.

That afternoon, I met up with Angie and Megan at Bahama Breeze. Normally, I would order the habanero wings with their special sauce, or the Caribbean Sea food special. But that moment wasn't so much about food. Least for Angie and me because Megan wasn't that enthused about meeting biological mother for the first time in years. And meeting a brother we had never even met. If it wasn't for Angie convincing her to be there. She would have never came.

Angie gave us a folder that had our biological mother's picture. I asked her what was her name she goes by because I had heard she changed her name within the years.

Megan said she didn't care to know what her name was then and she really didn't care what she had changed it to and for all she knew, she really didn't want to be there.

I thought I would pick with her, so I asked her why was she there and she said because Angie forced her to be there.

Angie said that we should all be there. If she went through the last year of locating her with all of the money she and Richard spent that we could a least meet out mother.

Megan said, you mean the crack head woman who threw us to the wolves. Angie asked Megan to hear her out. And to answer the question her name is Lisa.

Megan says, oh so she was a singer doing drugs…

I was hoping that Megan would just give up already. But I understood her frustration.

I asked Angie what was our brother name and she said his name was Sean and he was eighteen.

Megan said how sad that she kept one out of four.

Angie begged Megan's not to be rude when she arrive.

I looked at our mother's picture and I noticed that Angie looks like her the most. But Megan has her nose. Angie said that I had her hair and her eyes.

When I noticed our biological mother walking into the restaurant along with our younger brother. I had the OMG look on my face. We all stood up with maze. It was like another dream but only this time I knew it was real. Out of all of the placing and image of a small image to a larger image, why had I never thought about placing an image on my biological mother? Because I was dreaming all of that other stuff.

As our biological mother approached the table, Angie called her name out and hugged her. I was still in shock so I hugged her. She tried to hug Megan but Megan put the hands up didn't allow Lisa to touch her.

Angie asked her and our brother to please sit down and said, "You must be Sean." Sean said yes and you're Angie, and which one is Megan and Vivian.

I raised my hand and said I was Vivian and Megan turned her head. Sean said, he was really happy to meet us finally because his mother talked about us constantly.

Megan really turned away when she heard Sean speak about how his mother, which is our mother too would talk about us.

The look on Megan's face was a painful little kid because the whole time her head was turned.

When Angie told Sean that there wouldn't be any wonders again because all of Lisa's children have finally gotten together.

Lisa said that she never thought this day would have ever come. She knew that since the opportunity came for her to meet us as adults that she would need to explain herself.

I told Lisa that we knew some of what happened but not much. They only told us that we were taken away from you.

I let it be known that we found out about her doing drugs through other cruel children from the foster house because they had over heard our foster care parent talk about you.

Lisa apologized for everything and she knew that there was no way she could take back what we had gone through in those years and she said it with deep regret.

 Lisa also admitted to doing heavy drugs and said it was all true.

Meagan asked Lisa if she was still a drug attic. Lisa never got offended. But she did say that yes, she was still a recovering attic of nineteen years. And she praised God for her road to recovery.

Angie asked her why didn't she come for us afterwards. Lisa said that she was ashamed and she knew that we would have a much better life without her. Lisa was afraid of who she was at the time and had a hard time battling her demon she said.

Even when she was pregnant with Sean she was still doing drugs and a lot of other things. Until she was six months pregnant with Sean and beaten real bad and God gave her a second chance at living.

She said that each day she prayed for us and she prayed that we could someday forgive her. It was the glory of God that save her, She praises God each day and gives him the glory to protect us and that Sean did not become an attic baby.

I wanted to know if she had did drugs with any of she and us said no. She started doing drug right after she had all of us.

She said she joined church later on in life and she gave her life to Christ and she had changed and hoped that one day she would see us again.

Lisa explained to us how she had little help on getting us back because each time she tried to find out information on us she never got the help she needed and she was never able to afford an attorney so she gave up ten years after she had Sean.

Then Lisa said that we were all so beautiful. And she regrets loosing twenty-three years with us. Megan hollowed out and said twenty four years. I was four when you left us, even I know that. I bet you know everything about Sean huh.

Lisa told Megan she didn't leave them. That person she was at the time, caused the State to take them away from her. She admitted to being a horrible mother back then. But she has change now for the glory of God.

Megan told Sean that he was lucky because a least he had a mother there at all times.

Lisa asked Megan and each of us to forgive her and after our father was shot and killed she had gotten so bad off that she had us on the street with her from house to house and leaving us with strangers.

She explained to us that being an attic is a horrible disease to cure. Until she became a recovering attic and realized that she was creating her own monster world.

Angie told our biological mother that we should celebrate the fact of re uniting with her and not put to much negative energy in it and to let time heal our wombs.

I asked her where had she been living over the years. She said she had stayed in Phoenix for a while but not she lives in San Diego. Lisa grabbed Megan's hand and asked Megan to look her please.

She then began to tell Megan that her heart never stopped loving them for one minute and if it takes everyday of her life to repair the hurt and pain she has caused them she would dedicate that time and effort.

She asked Megan if they can a least start there.

Megan didn't have a problem with it; she just knew that it would take time to get to a friendship level with Lisa.

Angie sad good, now lets all order something to eat and talk about moving forward. Megan had softened up but she wasn't all of the way in to agreeing.

Angie told Sean that she would have loved to have grown up with a little brother. And by him being the youngest and so handsome she would have ran all of the little girls away from him.

Sean smile and said that she would have had a lot to run off because the honey sweat him like they having a workout. We all laughed and thought it was cute of him.

I told him that some day in life he will narrow it down to just one. Sean said yes Vivian that would be some day but no time soon, would I for see it.

Then he told Megan that he heard she likes to shop a lot at the nice places and he would love to hang out with her because beautiful honey's all shop and hang together.

You better believe that Sean saying those words to Megan made her crack a smile.

Megan told Sean that her friends were too old for him but he can hang out with her and maybe meet someone his own age.

Sean said that age didn't matter and he prefers them to be slightly older. Megan told him that a decade older is not slightly older. It was considered a big gap in age.

Sean said that he could mature up with his style. He could give a thirty year old man a run for his money and his honeys.

Little Sean had a lot of confidence and Megan knew she would enjoy him and the fact that there was her sibling who's younger than her. You couldn't tell me that those two wouldn't get along it was our biological mother and us that we had to work on. Between all of us, we had to pray on it.

CHAPTER 10

BEETHOVAN NIGHT

Going to the Opera House

After I met my biological mother, the other days had sailed by just normal. I had been back at the hospital to see my man and his condition was still the same.

I was beginning to live more than just being at the hospital all day every day. I would go by to see my man and talk to him and leave fresh flowers for him each day. I still didn't want him to wake up without me being there. But I believe that was what took me into those crazy dreams.

So it was Friday night. I had agreed to go to the Opera with Keven.

I pulled out a beautiful evening gown from my closet and I paired it up with the necklace my man had bought me one New Year's Eve.

Later that night of Opera

Later that night I was inside of the Limo with Keven. We were dressed for the evening.

Keven asked me if I was alright because I hardly said a word from the moment I stepped foot in the car.

I was fine that night. I might have been a little curious to going to such an elegant event. Not that I wasn't used to elegance. My man was pure elegance and I have hosted many events myself other than being an administrative assistant at somebody's fortune five hundred company.

But anyways, when we arrive house the lights on the Marquis were bright and beautiful.

Every classical song I have ever heard on movies and TV has played at the Opera House at one time or another.

A little kid growing up in the hood... it took me thirty-two years to experience something like this.

There goes to show you that its not where your from that defines you, its where your going and I stepped up in that Opera House like I belonged.

I thought that it was my man I was in the company of for a minute but it wasn't and that was okay because I was living me again.

I wanted to cry because I love my man so much and I didn't get a chance to share this experience with him first.

It wasn't fair to Keven how I felt inside but he didn't know how felt either. I wasn't allowing my book to be judged by its cover that night at all.

I was camera ready with a smile at all times and of course the cameras were flicking because Keven has fans.

I even heard one photographer saying, Black...hey Black over here. Keven turned toward the photographer so he could get a good snap picture of him.

I asked him silently, did that man just call you Black. Keven said yes. Black was his nick name when he played college basketball and the name Black carried on into his NBA years.

It felt good to have cameras all over us but they were there for Keven. Aka BLACK. I would have been nice for me to have signal people that way but please… maybe in another life.

I just know that night I felt so damn good.

Keven saw the necklace around my neck and he complimented it. I said thank you and I told him that it was a gift from my man a few years ago. He said it was such a lovely tasteful piece and that he admired my man taste.

Well he sure knew how to handle crap, because when I thought about it I said now come on woman, no man would want to keep hearing about my man who I love so much.

But Keven acted as if it never bothered him whenever I would say something about my man.

I knew it would only be fair to not bring my man up to Keven so often because that was something I would expect for Megan to do.

Then again we are sisters with the same blood running through our veins. I can't judge anybody.

After the cameras were done flicking, we stepped inside of the Auditorium where we had an exclusive seating area reserved for us.

I heard sound of a thunder and it scared me to the point where I jumped. Then the orchestra came from the ground up.

I said man, how many players are there? Keven said there could be about a hundred.

The conductor stretched his hands out for a few moments and there was complete silence in the air. Then in a flash, he led the orchestra.

The music sounded so good I wanted to get up and dance but Keven said no, that that wasn't the place to do that at. I was only kidding. I knew that.

By the time the singer came and her male actor I was in tears because all though I didn't know what the hell she was singing about, it sounded warm and touching and the male singer had me crying even more. Keven gave me a handkerchief and I could see that he was watching me through my peripheral vision.

What a beautiful night it was. It was more than what I had ever expected. The night at the Opera house ended with a big applause.

Outside of the Opera House

I didn't want the night to end there. So when Keven and I made it to the car I gave him a real shock when I asked him if I could go back to his place instead of the car dropping me off.

Keven said yes, but he was concerned with me being for sure if that was what I wanted to do. I couldn't get no more assured if someone had paid me to.

Later that night, Keven's house

When I got to Keven's house I admired his painting on the wall. He had a great big picture of a woman on his wall and he said it was his mother when she was in her twenties.

I was wowed by his place. It was big and beautiful.

His housekeeper came to give him a key she had found, and then she left.

I asked him if I could go for a tour in his house and he took me on a tour. By the time we made it to his living room I admired his piano.

He said when he was a kid that he wanted to play music but instead he had the love for basketball. But during his college days he majored in medicine to become a doctor and right soon after he had earned his degree he was drafted into the NBA.

So, with his first paycheck, he bought a baby grand piano and a house for his mother.

We went around different areas of his house and when I got to bedroom it was fixed up like a kings castle.

I was in complete admiration. I went over his bed and Keven was nobody's fool, he knew then what I wanted.

So I sat on Keven's bed and looked at him. He kneeled and reached down to take my shoes off. By then I already had his tie half way off.

I helped him as he pulled his jacket off and unbutton his shirt. When I saw his chest I sort of looked away but the body his body was irresistible. He then unzipped my dress from the back all the way down my spine.

I slipped my dress off and Keven pulled me upward on to the center of his bed.

Now I had gone that far but then I was hesitating to kiss him when he began to kiss me. Then I kissed him back passionately because I wanted to.

The rest of that moment was pure pleasure. It was so good that I was biting his sheets to keep from screaming. The way he held me when he stroked me in and out was similar to how my man does it to me when used to make love.

When it was all over Keven fell asleep. I put his shirt on and got up to look out of his bedroom window.

He woke up a sat up in his bed and asked me if I was okay. I was fine but I thought I should be going so I could get up and go the hospital the next morning.

Keven said it was the middle of the night and I should lie back down and rest a little until the morning. I did lie back down and slept like a baby.

When I woke up the next morning, Keven wasn't there. But there was breakfast made in the kitchen. I found some clothes to throw on from Keven's closet.

While I was eating a piece of toast Keven had come inside from a morning jog. He said he didn't want to wake me because I was calling the cows. I smiled and said I was sorry for snoring loud but I only snore when I'm dead tired.

Then he looked at me and said he see that I had found some clothes to put on. I told him it was all I could find. He said that I looked sexy in it and if I liked to I could stay for a while I could but I had to get going.

He asked if it was possible that he and I could go to dinner soon. At first, I was going to say, let me think about it, but then I said sure. We could do dinner and I said to let me know when it would be a good time for him. Keven said, that night.

I was thinking, but my man might wake up and was it wrong for me to have been there with Keven in the first place. Not to mention, I had sex with him and it was passionate sex to.

So I said okay. I would call to let him know what time was good.

CHAPTER 11

A SAD MOMENT

Later that afternoon I was okay but feeling guilty at the same time. Everything was back to normal. It had been almost two weeks now that my man had been in a coma. I had no delusional dreams of any sort.

I grabbed some flowers as always before I went up to his room. I smelled the flower and it smelled good. That day even the sun was shining. That was the first time since my man had been in a coma since the sun shined.

When I approached the ICU floor, the nurses and doctors walked by and smiled at me.

Just before I approached my man room I saw him come from his room and I smiled so big. But my man stopped and just stood there.

The closer I was to approaching him my smile was leaving my face. When I got up to him I said baby, you well. You're awake. My man kept looking down and I said what is it.

He looked up at me and I saw the doctor come out of my man room and pat my man on his shoulder as he walked past.

I asked my man to tell me what it was. He looked up at me and said that his blood work came back and said that he was positive and he needs a bone marrow. The Leukemia was affecting his organs and breaking his immune system down. And until he finds a match it wasn't much they could do but clean his blood periodically and eventually that might not help much.

Instantly, I dropped the flowers and I knew that I was in a dream. Then I heard the nurse call my name. I looked over at her and she asked me if I was alright. I shook my head and said no. I started crying and looked away from the nurse my man was gone from my presence.

I said where did he go and I heard the nurse say who, where did who go.

I was crying and walking slowly to my man room. I could hear my heart beat through my chest.

When I stepped foot in my man room. I saw him lying there still with the same condition. The nurse came inside with me and said he's right there Mrs. Eubanks.

I paused when she called me by a different last name and I looked at my hand and I realized that I was wearing a wedding ban.

So I proceeded to walk slowly by my man bedside and his face was bandaged up where I could only see his eyes.

I walked along side of his bed all the way around it to the other side.

Then I heard the nurse say to call her if I needed anything. I watched her leave and then I walked back around my man bed to get back to the other side of the bed but my eyes were still gazing him.

I looked at his heart monitor and I suddenly heard it beep louder. But it wasn't his heart monitor I was hearing, it was my heart I was hearing beep loud.

While I walked around his bed I touch his foot and I stopped. I stood at the foot of my man bed and I tuned around with my back facing him.

It was really odd but I aligned my body up to fit the way his body was laying in the bed.

I leaned back and felt my body falling slowly on to my man bed and I could still hear my heart beat and it was getting louder and louder.

All of a sudden, I was looking down at me lying in the hospital instead of being my man lying there.

I was standing there watching my body in that bed all bandaged up. Its like I was in a trans.

Although I wanted to move and get up I couldn't do anything. I couldn't even move as

I stood up watching my own self lay there in that bed.

The doctor walked in the room and walked right passed me and looked at me in the bed and grabbed my hand.

I head my man doctors voice and very clearly I hear him say, "We got movement" and to call the family.

When the doctor left out of the room, I followed him into the emergency room and then I saw them working on someone who had flat lined.

All I heard was clear... there were about three other people surrounding this person trying to revive him.

After a minute, I saw the doctor shake his head and everyone took their mask off and left the room.

I didn't understand what was happening but I needed to wake up.

I pulled my face but I still didn't wake up. Just as I was about to walk over to see who that person was on the table who had flat line I heard someone call my name. So I turned away without even looking at that person body and when I got back into the hallway, I saw the nurse and paramedic rushing someone in with an IV attached to their body.

They brushed passed me and it was my body they were out to save.

Still I knew I was only dreaming so I said out loud and walking with the everyone while they were rushing the stretcher trying to get it to a room.

I asked, why am I in there. No one was hearing me. I said it again while still walking along the side of the stretcher, why am I in that stretcher.

No one answered. The nurse pulled the stretcher over to the side with me still laying there unconscious on the stretcher.

Then she went over and tried to whisper to the doctor. I heard the nurse tell the doctor there was a crash and that the sister was trying to get her sister's husband hear before the collision happened. He had Leukemia and his body gave out at right after dinner.

Then I heard the worse words of my life. I heard the nurse say to the doctor that the husband was dead on arrival and the sister who was the driver was being ex-rayed for any internal bleeding but their didn't seemed to be life threaten injuries.

Then I heard the doctor say, and her. Talking about me next and I listened in closure to see exactly what the nurse was saying.

So the nurse said she lost a lot of blood and we already put in for a blood transfer. We don't know at this point.

Then suddenly I saw Megan wheeled out in a wheel chair and I went up to Megan and said Megan, tell me what happened. Megan looked at me and started crying and saying how sorry she was.

Then I heard some people voices in my man room.

So I left Megan sitting in the chair and walked toward my man room. By the time I had made it to the door I saw everyone standing over the bed talking to my man.

So I walked slowly and walked in between them and as I approached the bed it was me lying in the bed.

I heard my sister Angie's voice saying. OMG she's opening her eyes. I heard Richard's mother say, yes Lord thank you Jesus.

When I opened my eyes I didn't see me standing around by the bed side anymore.

The lights from the ceiling of the hospital room were too bright for my eyes so everything seemed blurry.

When I was finally able to get a clear vision, I was looking straight ahead.

I heard the doctor say, Vivian can you hear me. Can you hear me Vivian.

I shook my head a little bit. I looked over to my left and the first person I saw was my sister Angie. She was crying and holding her hand in her chest. I reached out to grab her hands.

I was wondering if I was in a dream because it seemed so real to see my family there.

Then I saw Richard and he smiled at me. Then I tried to talk. It felt like I almost forgot how to talk.

Then I remembered how to talk and I asked if Megan was okay.

Megan pushed her way through and said, honey I'm fine, you know I like to party but my sister was much more important than me being out.

Then she leaned over and said, I made my boyfriend come with me tonight and he's African. A Nigerian African.

I looked over and saw Megan's boyfriend standing in the background. He nodded his head and smiled at me.

I guess that was him because everyone else I knew. Then I saw Lisa and my younger brother Sean.

I said to Angie, you found our mom. Lisa came over and held my hand to.

Then Angie said to me, Vivian, Dr, Duvall called us and we all ran over here as quickly as we could.

I said doctor Duvall, Kevin and Doctor Duvall said yes Vivian. I looked at the doctor and it was Keven. My Keven.

I said Keven, why are you here? Megan beat him to the punch and answered the question.

She said, thank God he was here. He was hear everyday side by side with you. Honey Dr. Duvall is the best doctor I've ever known.

Then Megan leaned over to me and said it so everyone could hear her this time and said, If

you ask me I would think that you and the
Doctor had known each other before you
crashed your car and ended up here.
Especially the way he's been here day in and
day out. And Sis girl, he is hella fine.

So then I asked Angie if I was ever married
before and Angie looked over at the doctor and
said Dr. Duvall, is my sister going to be okay.

Dr. Duvall looked at Vivian and said, she's
going to be just fine. It takes a few days
sometimes when the brain has rested for days.

Angie looked back at me and sad, Yes Vivian.
You were married to Tie remember, before he
passed of Leukemia five years ago.

I knew that already. But I also knew that once
I had asked her that question and she'd answer
yes as she did, then this was a for real moment.
And I knew that I was back to normal and
alive and well.

Then the doctor came over and said, I know
this is against NSODC, but I would love to

marry you Vivian and if you would say yes, I would be the happiest man on earth.

Before I was able to say yes I saw my Niece Reign come from behind her father Richard and said, Happy New Year's Ante Vivian, I brought you a flower.

Tear fell from my eyes and I looked at Dr. Kevin Duvall and said yes, I will.

Megan said, that's right and turned the TV on. The ball was about to be dropped in New York City and my family all started to count down into the New Year.

All I heard was ten, nine, eight, seven, six, five, four, three, two, one. The big HAPPY NEW YEAR.

Chapter 12

CLOSURE

Sitting in Dr. Halle Robinson's office

I was lying on doctor Halle couch. And she said that she feel that this should be our last session but of course if I wanted to continue to see her that I could.

Dr. Halle said that she feel that now I have closure. Since the death of my ex – man and the life of happiness which my new man has brought me.

I have closure and I was going to be just fine now that we have gone through my entire life and why I had my Heraldry moments.

I said you know Dr. Halle, the killing part about this whole thing is, I found through an ex-girlfriend of my ex-husband that his nickname was Tie. And I found out through a fan/photographer that my husband now nick name is BLACK.

Dr, Halle said she knows because I have told her that about a thousand times and she feels that there must have been something to the two men I love the most.

Then she reached over behind her desk and gave me a gift and asked me to open it.

When I opened the box, it was a gift of a Man's BLACK TIE. A gorgeous Black Tie.

Dr. Halle said that I could give it to my man or I could keep it forever and frame it. She said to think of it as a symbol of Black and Tie because one was a great man in my life and the other waiting outside of her door is a wonderful man in my life now.

She said she thought about me when she went to Bloomingdales and thought since I talked about Tie and Black so much that she would buy me a Black Tie to live with forever.

One thing for sure she said she had never known or ever heard about a man being as strong as my man. She said that there needed to be more men like Dr. Kevin Duvall out there in the world.

I sat up on of the couch I told Dr. Halle that my man was the best thing that has ever happened for me and I thanked Dr. Halle for listening to me.

As I was getting up Dr. Halle offered to help me but I asked her not to.

Dr. Halle then opened the door to let Keven know that his wife was ready.

I reached over to grab my crutches and Keven came in with the wheelchair.

I sat inside the wheelchair and Dr. Halle asked me to take care of myself.

Keven said, don't worry…I got her!

Jara Everett

THE END

Rest in Peace

In honor of my cousin

Tillman Clayborne Stallion

January 29, 1975 – September 16, 2014

ACKNOWLEDGMENTS

God, My dear family, Printhouse Books.

Follow me:
Facebook: Jaraeverett and Jara
             Everett Official
Twitter: Jara Everett
Instagram: The realjaraeverett

Thank you for reading; Black Tie; check out other titles from Jara Everett and more at www.Printhousebooks.com

Jara Everett; Hip Hop's Mistress releases her first Tell all Auto Biography; taking you on a journey into the world of Hip Hop and Entertainment from Chicago, Miami, LA to Atlanta. You will experience laughter, disbelief and erotic pleasures as she shares her experiences with R. Kelly, Suge Knight, Tupac,

Martin Lawrence, Young Jeezy, Shawty Redd, Jazze Pha, Too Short, Gary Busey and more in this epic tell all; adequately titled Jumpoff !

PRINTHOUSE BOOKS

Read it, Enjoy it, Tell a friend.

VIP INK Publishing Group, Incorporated.

Atlanta, GA.

www.PrintHouseBooks.com